THE RETREAT

Alison Moore's first novel, *The Lighthouse*, was shortlisted for the Man Booker Prize and the National Book Awards (New Writer of the Year), winning the McKitterick Prize. Both *The Lighthouse* and her second novel, *He Wants*, were *Observer* Books of the Year. Her short fiction has been included in *Best British Short Stories* and *Best British Horror* anthologies, broadcast on BBC Radio 4 Extra and collected in *The Pre-War House and Other Stories*. Born in Manchester in 1971, she lives near Nottingham with her husband Dan and son Arthur.

ALSO BY ALISON MOORE

NOVELS
The Lighthouse (2012)
He Wants (2014)
Death and the Seaside (2016)
Missing (2018)

SHORT STORIES
The Pre-War House and Other Stories (2013)

CHILDREN'S FICTION
Sunny and the Ghosts (2018)
Sunny and the Hotel Splendid (2019)
Sunny and the Wicked Lady (2020)

THE RETREAT

ALISON MOORE

SALT

CROMER

PUBLISHED BY SALT PUBLISHING 2021

2 4 6 8 10 9 7 5 3 1

First published in Great Britain in 2021 by
Salt Publishing Ltd
12 Norwich Road, Cromer, Norfolk NR27 0AX United Kingdom

www.saltpublishing.com

Salt Publishing Limited Reg. No. 5293401

A CIP catalogue record for this book is available from the British Library

ISBN 978 1 78463 221 2 (Paperback edition)
ISBN 978 1 78463 222 9 (Electronic edition)

Typeset in Neacademia by Salt Publishing

Printed and bound in Great Britain by Clays Ltd, Elcograf S.p.A

For Penny and Sarah

PROLOGUE

L IEL WAS AN in-between place. Lying one hundred miles from the English coast, the island resembled Sandra's known world but it had its own currency and its own system of car number plates; its post boxes were blue and its telephone boxes were yellow. It was not far from France but was not French. The island had its own distinctive language but Sandra had only heard English spoken there, though in a foreign accent. Some of the street signs and house names were in English and some were in French, or at least it looked like French. She did not, when she first holidayed there, know much French. At school, she learnt to say Je suis une fille unique, which sounded better than it was, and J'ai un cochon d'Inde, although she did not have one. Later still, she learnt phrases from a book: Good morning and Good afternoon, and I must go now and Go away! She could say A table for one please and I didn't order this and Can I have a refund? She could say Can you help me? and I'm really sorry and I don't understand. She imagined herself stranded with these phrases, hoping she would be all right.

It was from the dining room window of Liel's Sea View hotel that Sandra first saw the smaller island of Lieloh, sunlit on the horizon. It looked like the dome of a sea monster's head, as if it were crouched on the seabed and might suddenly rise up. 'What's that?' she asked. Her mother put down her butter knife and turned to look. She said it was only an island

and that Sandra should finish her soup. 'But what island is it?' asked Sandra. Her mother said it must be Lieloh and that her soup would go cold. Sandra, stirring her soup, said, 'Can we go there?' Her mother said they had almost finished their holiday and that they already had plans for their remaining days, and her father added that it would not have been possible anyway because the island was privately owned and if she did not finish her soup it would be taken away and then she would be hungry. Sandra lifted a spoonful of soup towards her mouth, then lowered it to ask, 'Who owns it?' Her father said Lieloh belonged to the Swansons, who were very rich. Valerie Swanson had been in films, said her mother, although she had to be in her sixties by now, and in her retirement was living on her own island in a house of her own design; and she was famous for her lavish parties, to which only artists were invited. Sandra pictured Valerie Swanson, star of the silver screen, sleek haired, silk gowned, standing in the doorway of her mansion, or on a patio looking out at her extensive and immaculate garden, or on a balcony watching the sun set, as her party guests mingled. Her mother said boats were seen out there, and Sandra imagined them dotted around the island like moons around an alien planet, haunting the shore like the boats that gathered outside Brigitte Bardot's beach house, hoping to catch a glimpse of her. But, added her mother, looking at the undisturbed view, there didn't seem to be any there now.

The closest Sandra could get to Lieloh was to walk along the sea front and down to the docks. Through binoculars, she could see trees, and she thought of the island of happiness, which no longer appeared on maps but whose hills and woods, and glimpses of chimneys and curls of smoke, had been described by an antiquarian who had seen with his own eyes this island where contentment was assured. Sandra had read all about it, but could not remember where it was said to be. Somewhere beyond that barrier of greenery was the home that Valerie Swanson had built with her film-star earnings. Sandra took a photograph, but when she got back to the mainland and had her pictures processed, Lieloh just looked like dark clouds on the horizon.

In adulthood, she honeymooned on Liel. Alex had suggested a smart hotel in the middle of the island, but Sandra wanted something further out; she wanted to stay in the Sea View. She agreed that it was old-fashioned but it was right on the coast, and every morning they woke to the sound and smell of the sea and the squawk of the gulls, which Alex said would drive them mad. At the dining room window, Sandra looked for Lieloh as if not entirely expecting to find that it was still there, as if it might turn out to have been a childhood invention or a mirage, but there it was. She pointed it out to Alex, but he did not see the attraction. It was rather small, he said, and far away. He felt, perhaps, the same way she did whenever he drew her attention to babies and toddlers and told her how nice it would be to have one of their own, to have a family. 'I've always wanted children,' he said, 'haven't you?' She hadn't really, and had not thought much about it. She had never even held a baby.

Once upon a time, she had wanted to go to art college, to become an artist. She had won certificates for her art at school, and, in her final year, a prize for the greatest effort. But it was a precarious kind of life; as an artist, she might struggle to support herself. She ended up in an office, on reception, but around the edges of her workday she sometimes thought about making some art, and might sketch the mug she'd just drunk from, or the ketchup bottle, still life; she tried sketching the cat but had trouble with anything that moved. Occasionally, the start of a new year prompted her to sign up for an evening class. The one with which she struggled most was life drawing, to the point that she felt compelled to apologise to the life model for mangling him. He didn't care, he said; he was only there to make some cash. He told her he was really an actor, and that he was going to go to LA; he was going to get into films. She smiled, remembering her own teenage daydreams, and told him she had once thought of going to art college and becoming an artist.

'You should,' he said.

'Do you think so?' she asked, looking sceptically at her work.

He shrugged again and said, 'If that's what you want. It isn't too late. Live the dream!'

She said it was impossible – how was she supposed to live? She had a mortgage and bills to pay; she had responsibilities at home and the possibility of a promotion at work.

At the final class, before he left for LA, he said, 'Look out for me.'

Years later, finally deciding that she had no talent for people, life drawing, portraiture, she bought her first water-colour kit and took a watercolour seascapes class, whose only downside was that the classroom was in a building that could hardly have been further from the sea. When she and Alex returned to Liel, she took her kit with her, and discovered an artists' group that was open to holidaymakers, and to anyone who felt inclined to drop in. She devoted some hours to working alongside them in a community centre, while Alex went sightseeing alone. It was jolly and friendly but vaguely unsatisfying and she felt that was because she and everyone else were free to drop in and out, to come and go. She wanted

4

something more committed. During a coffee break, she sat flipping through a magazine featuring artists and musicians and writers, all of them young and beautiful, and articles accompanied by gorgeous illustrations: flowers and clothes and abstract designs; a night sky to accompany an item on astronomy; bare branches framing a piece about gloves; a Welsh beach scene whose colours were glorious, the cold greys of the lowering sky and the sea turning to white against the earth tones of the headland, and on the sand, the little figures of a family, hand in hand, walking away, their shadows long behind them. Sandra imagined the artist labouring over this artwork in her own studio, at a desk at a window with plenty of light, with a kettle and a jar of coffee nearby, and a cat, there always had to be a cat. That would be her ideal job, she thought. She turned the page, and came face-to-face with an advert for an artists' retreat on the island of Lieloh. She stared, hardly believing her eyes. There was a picture of the house. It was not exactly a mansion but it was a big house, and attractive, its walls eggshell-blue and sunlit, its aspidistra-green front door framed by a rose arch. She tore out the advert, to show Alex this invitation to visit an island that for so long had been out of bounds.

'I guess Valerie Swanson must be dead by now,' said Alex.

'I wonder what it's like,' said Sandra, 'living on an island.'

'You live on an island,' said Alex. 'Britain's an island.'

'Yes,' said Sandra. And she had stayed on Liel a few times. But she was thinking of somewhere smaller, somewhere unspoilt; she was thinking of Lieloh. She was looking at the advert, at the PO Box number to which bookings could be sent.

1

CAROL IS GOING to miss the city. She will miss the theatres and the restaurants and the bars. She has favourites but most of all she appreciates the variety, the choice. There is always some new venue or show opening, and a friend to go with. The cinema is advertising a film that she would have liked to see but which has not yet been released. She will have to watch it some other time, at home, on her little TV.

She will even miss the buskers, she thinks, dropping some change into a music student's open violin case.

She doubts she will miss the crowds, the pavements choked with meandering pedestrians who, as the rain starts, open umbrellas whose spokes go for her eyes.

She will not miss the prices, the tourist tat, the congestion, the dirty air. She will not miss this weather. The puddles are spoiling her new calfskin shoes, wetting her tights. But then, she supposes, the weather will be much the same where she is going.

She will miss her son, of course. She will miss Jayne, and their lunches, during which Jayne listens patiently while Carol complains. Mostly, she complains that, although her short stories are well-received, she is almost unknown, and that the novel she has always wanted to write is still not written. She writes fantasy. What she really wants is to write a series of fantasy novels.

Carol keeps reading interviews in which an author will

say that their novel *came quite easily*, that *it wrote itself*. But a novel does not write itself. *She* writes her novel. Or rather, she thinks – dashing between two cars, ignoring the honking – she does not.

It just seemed to fall out of me. They make it sound like childbirth, during which she knows there must have been pain because she had to ask for an epidural, but she cannot remember the pain itself, what it felt like. There were hours and hours of labour but they have concertinaed in her mind. She knows she tore badly and vomited repeatedly but mostly what she remembers is the baby landing on her chest, and her holding, both very suddenly and at the end of nine long months, this surprising life. Her third-degree tear has long since healed and is invisible to her now. She never did give her little boy a sibling.

Now it's just her – with her son grown and gone, and her husband gone, and even the dog's heart finally giving out – she could have a little flat, that would be enough. She could grow flowers in a window box, go for strolls, see Jayne, visit her son and his family, read gossip magazines and other people's bestsellers, cook and bake and sleep well. But: she wants to write. She wants to write the novel that for years she has been talking about writing. She wants to appear in window displays. She wants to be translated and read around the world. She wants a Netflix series, or to see her work on the big screen. She does have ideas, and she does get started, but she finds it desperately hard to really get anywhere, and then it is too easy to give in to distractions.

She steps aside now, out of the crowd, out of the rain, into the peace and comfort of the restaurant in which Jayne is waiting to hear her news.

2

LEAVING HOME WITH her rucksack and a satchel, Sandra feels as if she were going on a school trip, as if she ought to have labelled her belongings, to have 'SANDRA PETERS' sewn into all her clothes, including her underwear; or she feels, closing the front door quietly because it is still early, as if she were running away.

She drives herself to the airport, leaves her car in the long-stay car park and catches a late morning flight from the mainland to Liel. Outside Liel airport, she waits in the rain for a bus that will take her to the south coast. There is no shelter, just the stop. She puts up her hood. When the bus arrives, she requests a single to the port and settles into a seat near the front. She watches the rain spattering against the window and thinks *Here I am, on my way to Lieloh*. She smiles at the thought. Here she is, on her way to live in Valerie Swanson's house, among artists, in a little community. She imagines them supporting and inspiring one another, fetching vegetables from a kitchen garden, cooking together. She wonders what they will be like, these strangers with whom she will be spending the coming fortnight.

Near the port, the houses become smaller and more functional: single-storey boxes, with plain doors and windows with storm shutters. The Sea View hotel stands alone, looking decorative and fussy beside the houses, and more exposed. This is where Sandra will put up, before catching the midweek ferry to Lieloh.

She climbs the damp stone steps to the foyer. The receptionist has been there for years, in the same outdated uniform. 'Yes, here you are,' she says, finding Sandra's booking on the computer, handing over the key to a room that turns out to lack a sea view. It could be worse though, and it's only for one night.

When Sandra wakes on the Wednesday morning, it takes her a moment to get her bearings. She opens the curtains and sees sunshine, though it is cold enough, she realises later, for a jumper. She has a good breakfast in the dining room and then returns to her bedroom and puts on the television news until it is time to check out. The Turner Prize exhibition is opening at the Tate. The shortlisted work includes an unmade bed which Sandra, sitting on her own unmade bed, does not feel she understands.

Her flat shoes are quiet on the paving slabs as she walks to the docks, picking up a sandwich on the way. She has been instructed to wait at the top of the furthest ramp, to catch the noon ferry. She can see a ferry at the bottom of the ramp. It is smaller than she was expecting but it is bound to be hers.

Sandra sits down on a bench and waits, full of the nervous excitement she feels before job interviews (during which she is likely, perhaps as soon as she enters the room, or perhaps when the interview is nearly over, to commit a faux pas, to say the wrong thing, to give the wrong impression) or dates, though it's a long time since she went on one of those.

'Are you here for the retreat?'

Sandra turns to see who has spoken. A tall woman in a cheerful orange coat is taking a seat on the bench. 'Yes,' says Sandra. She smiles and adds, 'I like your orange coat.'

'Thank you,' says the woman. 'It's apricot.' She turns to look at the ferry and asks, 'Is that the ferry to Lieloh?'

'I think so,' says Sandra.

Others are gathering now. There are two more women, who are standing together, and Sandra thinks *Spiker and Sponge*. Sponge looks heavily pregnant. Spiker has an expensive rucksack boasting sewn-on patches from all over the world, from cities and countries and continents that Sandra has never been to, and she speaks with a confidence that would prompt Sandra's mother to say, as a disapproving aside, 'She's very sure of herself.'

And there are two men: one baby-faced in a camouflage jacket and combat trousers, the other bigger and hairier and ruddier, optimistically dressed in a tropical shirt and shorts and eating a packet of cheese and onion crisps.

'This is the first time I've been off the mainland,' says Sponge, sitting down on the other side of Sandra. She has a nasal voice and reeks of cigarette smoke.

'It's not my first time,' says the man in the holiday clothes, 'but it's my first time alone.'

'You're not alone,' says Sponge. 'You're with us.'

He tells them he's left his wife and children, and Spiker says, 'They'll be all right. I've left my husband with two teenage boys and three dogs.'

'No,' says the man, 'I mean, I've left them for good.'

'Oh, I see,' says Spiker.

'It might not be for good,' says Sponge. 'You might go back.'

'No,' he says, shaking his head. 'I won't go back. I made my choice.'

Sponge turns to Sandra and asks where she's come from. Sandra mentions her home town, which Sponge says she's never heard of. 'It's a nice place,' says Sandra, who had a happy childhood, in a house with a long garden with a stream at the bottom, but she couldn't wait to leave. She lives in the suburbs now, with Alex, in a comfortable semi; they sometimes talk about escaping, but he just means for the weekend.

'Have you been to Liel before?' asks Sponge.

'I've been here on holiday,' says Sandra.

'I couldn't live on Liel,' says Spiker. 'It's too quiet for me.'

'It looked nice in pictures,' says Sponge. 'All beaches and sunsets.'

Sandra nods. 'It's lovely in the summer.'

'It's not how I imagined,' says Sponge.

'It's too quiet,' insists Spiker.

'And rather cold,' says Sponge.

'Lieloh should be interesting though,' says the woman in the apricot coat.

'The house looked nice in the picture,' says Sponge.

It would be her dream life, says Sandra; the retreat would be a taste of a perfect way of living. She begins to explain to them her vision of this group as a kind of artists' colony, a community of artists supporting and inspiring one another, but they are being summoned. The six of them descend the ramp to the ferry, where men are waiting to take them across. The ferryman, who stands at the gangplank to help them aboard, is youngish but weather-beaten, with close-cropped brown hair and a new-looking khaki anorak zipped up against the elements. The other man counts them, as if in a group this small it might be possible to lose someone.

They find seats. The crossing from Liel to Lieloh will take less than an hour; it is not that far away, perhaps ten miles. It is too far to swim to – Sandra, at least, who tires after twenty lengths of the local pool, could not swim even half a mile in one go.

Sandra takes a seat next to the woman in the apricot coat, who says, as the ferry pulls out of the harbour, 'I've never spent so long with strangers.'

'Well, we won't be strangers for long,' says Sandra. 'We'll get to know one another soon enough.'

'I'm Harriet,' says the woman.

'I'm Sandra,' says Sandra, pleased to have made her first friend among the group.

'Don't be offended if I don't remember that,' says Harriet. 'I'm terrible with names.'

The rumble of the engine and the gentle rocking of the boat is soporific. Sandra lets her eyes close and turns her face up to the sun, until she starts to feel woozy.

'What do you do?' asks Harriet, as Sandra opens her eyes.

'I'm a visual artist,' says Sandra.

'I mean,' says Harriet, 'what do you do for a living?'

'Oh,' says Sandra. 'I'm a receptionist.' It's all right. It's not very satisfying but then it's not very stressful either. Although sometimes it *is* stressful, when people are complaining, when they're angry, and Sandra, behind the reception desk, feels cornered, *is* physically cornered, trying to keep her tone cool. 'What about you?'

Harriet mentions the university at which she works, which is attached to an art gallery at which Sandra once saw an exhibition. It was an exhibition of sculptures that Sandra had been keen to see but which she felt, when she stood looking at them, she failed to understand. 'That's a common response,' says Harriet, who visited the same exhibition and has written about the artist's work.

Sandra suggests sharing a room in the house on Lieloh, but Harriet says no. 'I paid for a single room,' she says. 'I don't know about the others, apart from the men - the men have been put together.' Sandra looks across at the other women, at Spiker and Sponge. They both seem friendly enough.

Everyone sets about eating whatever they have brought with them for lunch, though Sandra leaves most of her sandwich, putting it away in her rucksack for later: the soporific rocking has developed into a violent tipping sensation that makes her stomach feel like it's falling through her feet, as if she were on some terrible ride at the funfair. She is acutely aware of the miles and miles of cold, dark sea into which she would not want to drop.

The ferry rises and falls, and rises and falls, on the relentless green-grey waves.

3

JAYNE IS WAITING for Carol in the restaurant's conservatory, where the branches of cherry-blossom trees reach along the walls and across the ceiling. It is like a stage set for A Midsummer Night's Dream; it is like Max's bedroom in Where the Wild Things Are. The trees are not real of course; the cherry blossom is not real.

There is jazz playing in the background, which Carol finds soothing. She joins Jayne at a table for two near the fireplace. There is a good fire going and the warmth just about reaches them.

'Look at my shoes,' says Carol, showing Jayne the damp calfskin, her damp tights.

Jayne sympathises. She has ordered wine, she says. They both know the wine here is good; if there's one thing Carol cannot bear, it is substandard wine.

They browse the menu, and a waiter brings their drinks and takes their food order. Carol asks for the duck foie gras followed by the venison. They sip their glasses of pinot noir and Jayne says, 'So tell me your news.'

Carol has been putting off this moment, knowing that her friend will try to change her mind, but it's too late now, there will be no talking her out of it.

'You've written your novel?' prompts Jayne.

'No,' says Carol.

'No,' says Jayne, 'I was joking.'

'I'm going away for a while,' says Carol.

'That sounds ominous,' says Jayne.

Carol laughs. She butters her bread and says, 'Do you remember Roman?'

'Roman with the good looks and the private island?' says Jayne, making eyes at her friend. 'I do indeed.'

'That's where I'm going,' says Carol.

Jayne is agog. 'You're going to stay with Roman on his private island?'

'Roman isn't living there,' says Carol. 'He wants to sell it, but he offered me the chance to stay in the empty house in the meantime.'

'You mean you're going to stay there alone?' says Jayne.

'That's the idea,' says Carol. 'It's the perfect place to try and write my novel. There'll be no distractions.'

'No Jayne,' says Jayne. 'No boozy lunches. No lost afternoons.'

'I'll have nothing to do but write,' says Carol. She expects Roman will visit her though; she would hope to have a little bit of company from time to time.

'You're going to lock yourself away in a room,' says Jayne, 'and not come out until you've spun all the straw into gold.'

'Something like that,' says Carol.

'How long are you going for?' asks Jayne.

'As long as it takes,' says Carol.

'As long as it takes to sell the island or as long as it takes to write the novel?' asks Jayne.

'Either way,' says Carol, 'at the end of it, either I'll return with a finished novel or I won't.'

'You'll hate it,' says Jayne, as the waiter arrives with their meals.

Carol smiles at her friend and picks up her cutlery.

'But you can always phone me,' says Jayne. 'I'll come and get you. In my private helicopter.'

They both laugh, while the fire dances in the grate and the rain hammers down outside.

4

TRYING TO FEEL a little less sick, less green around the gills, Sandra moves to the front of the boat. Standing at the bow, dashed by the sea spray and battered by the wind, she feels like Kate Winslet in Titanic, which won about a dozen Oscars last year, though not Best Actress.

Almost there. Sandra watches the island getting closer, getting bigger, though the house remains hidden: beyond the trees, she cannot see so much as a roof, so much as chimney pots, or curls of smoke rising into the sky.

The ferryman brings the boat in carefully, mooring it alongside the jetty, and the passengers disembark with their luggage. The man who counted them gets off too, saying, 'Welcome to Lieloh.' He turns away to help the ferryman unload the packages he has brought across.

'It's even colder here than it is on Liel,' says Sponge, shivering on the dock. She reaches into her coat pocket, takes out her cigarettes and lights up. The smoke wreathes towards Sandra, who moves, trying to keep out of its way.

It is peaceful enough, apart from the birds – the circling gulls, and others calling from the trees. The man in the camouflage jacket listens carefully, trying to identify the birdsong. 'That sounds very much like a red-backed shrike,' he says, 'though it doesn't seem likely.'

'Aren't they extinct?' says Harriet.

'Virtually,' says the man. 'In Britain anyway. Perhaps not here.'

'Are we not still in Britain?' asks Sponge.

'No,' says Spiker, 'we're not.'

Sponge looks perturbed, as if, without her passport or inoculations, she has stepped into another world by mistake. She checks that they are still in the same time zone, and seems to take some comfort from that.

They stand facing the trees, listening to the distant birdsong. The man explains the etymology of the word 'shrike', from the Old English for 'shriek', referring to the bird's shrill call, but to Sandra it sounds perfectly pretty, entirely charming.

She has been thinking of the trees as a screen, like the leylandii that neighbours squabble over, but now she is closer she can see that the woodland is quite extensive, with a dirt track cutting through it.

While the ferryman smokes a cigarette, the other man goes to a ramshackle outbuilding next to the dirt track and fetches a buggy – it is electric, eerily quiet. He brings it to the jetty and lifts in the items that came over on the ferry.

Sponge has got out a mobile phone. After frowning at the screen, she holds it up in the air, and then higher still, trying to find a signal. 'You won't get a signal here,' says the man, who is loading their luggage in now. There's no landline either, they've been told that. Sandra is looking forward to the absence of ringing phones. In case of emergency, there's a radio, but it's not like this is a shooting trip; someone might suffer a paper cut, or a twisted ankle, that's about it. Unless Sponge is really dangerously pregnant, and in that case why would she come here? And unless someone does something daft.

The man explains that he will take everything up to the house in the buggy. They can follow on foot, it's not far. 'I've got room for one in the passenger seat,' he adds, getting into the driver's seat, leaving them to fight it out among themselves. Sandra is closest, but Spiker says to Sponge, 'You should take it.' Sponge thanks her, drops her cigarette butt and, holding onto her belly, climbs in. The man turns the buggy around and sets off – driving rather fast, thinks Sandra, but she can't talk: she goes too fast at times, and once crashed her car into a tree. She was treated for shock, but in a way it was inevitable.

Those left behind follow quickly – Sandra thinks of the children of Hamelin pursuing the Pied Piper – except for the smaller man who keeps stopping to poke around in the undergrowth.

'We're going to have a fantastic time here,' says Sandra. When no one replies, she adds, 'I believe there are puffins.'

Beneath the trees, dropped needles and fallen leaves form a carpet, decomposing underfoot. Beyond the woodland, the dirt track is bare, and rough enough that Sandra must watch her step. Hedge-lined, with moorland on either side, the track is reminiscent of lanes she knows in Derbyshire, except that this moorland gives way to the sea. She thinks of Stanley Royle's 'Morning on the Derbyshire Moors', his woman in white gazing out across the sunlit heather. In an article, Sandra read that this figure was his wife, who had, at the time of painting, been taken into a mental hospital for what would now be recognised as post-natal depression. Lodge Moor was mentioned, but that, when Sandra looked it up, appeared to be an isolation hospital.

The dirt track brings them to the house, which Sandra had imagined standing quite alone in the middle of the island, but there are various ugly outbuildings in the vicinity, one with pebble-dashed walls, another with a corrugated metal roof. The house itself, though, looks just as it did in the advert in the glossy magazine, except that from this angle she can see, attached to the roof tiles, the black slabs of solar panels; and the sun's gone in, dulling the pale blue walls; and up close there are signs of neglect – there are cracks in the plaster, and the paint on the front door is peeling, and the rose arch needs deadheading, and all in all the house does not look quite as picturesque as it did in the advert. Several knotty apple trees are growing in front of the house, and Sandra thinks of *The Wizard of Oz*, of Dorothy picking an apple from a tree that slaps her hand and takes its apple back.

Leaving the buggy in the middle of the track, the man lets the group into the house. In the spacious hallway, the six of them hang their coats on the half-dozen pegs and line up their boots on the stone-tiled floor, and Sandra, in her socks, thinks *I'm standing in Valerie Swanson's hallway.* The tiles extend into the kitchen, whose centrepiece is a farmhouse table around which they gather.

'You cater for yourselves,' says the man. He shows them where everything is – 'Fridge, cellar, garden . . .' – gesturing like a flight attendant pointing out the emergency exits. There is fresh and long-life milk, fresh and frozen bread and vegetables, fruit in a bowl and growing outside, dried pasta and rice, dried and tinned pulses, a full wine rack, and enough meat and ice cream in the chest freezer to last them for months let alone weeks. Had this been a survival scenario, they could have done worse.

'Some of you have brought supplies of your own,' he observes, as the man in the tropical shirt opens another packet of cheese and onion crisps. 'If you want to order extra bakery items, you can do that through me.' He takes a sheet of paper out of his back pocket and reads through a list: 'Macaroni cheese pie, buttermilk pie, egg custard tarts, treacle scones, brandy buns, caramel cream puffs, brown sugar sponge, tipsy cake. Who wants what?' He takes the group's orders. Only Sandra abstains; everything sounds so rich, so sickly.

She gazes through the window into the garden, which is disappointingly drab. Close to the house, the lawn has been slabbed to make a bleak patio. There is no kitchen garden, nothing like that, just more of those apple trees. Back on the mainland, she has herbs in pots on the windowsills, though they block the light. Alex will be watering them while she's gone.

The smell of the cheese and onion crisps is getting to Sandra. She wanders across the hallway into the lounge, thinking that the stone floor could do with a rug. Apart from that, she can imagine this being quite cosy: sofas and armchairs are arranged around a long coffee table on whose polished surface sits a hardback *History of Art*. In addition to this, an ambitious collection of expensive art books fills a whole wall of bookshelves, except for a few inches given over to thin volumes of poetry and other miscellany. Sandra marvels at the fact that she is in Valerie Swanson's home, touching things that Valerie Swanson must have touched with her film-star hands. She can see some Mapplethorpes up on the top shelf, out of her reach, as if this were a newsagent's and she were too young, not yet ready, to see such things.

It is so quiet. At home, there is always someone wanting something. Here, alone, or as good as alone, she can really start to work.

By the time she realises that everyone else has taken their luggage and gone upstairs, most of the beds have been claimed.

There are two large twin rooms at the back of the house, overlooking the garden. The men have installed themselves in one and Sponge is unpacking in the other. There are two more rooms at the front of the house, overlooking the dirt track. Harriet is in one and Spiker has got the other. When Sandra opens a fifth door at the top of the stairs, she finds the bathroom. From the doorway of the twin room, she says to Sponge, 'Room for one more?'

'The more the merrier,' says Sponge as Sandra comes in. 'As long as you've no bad habits.'

The room is shockingly white, from the walls and floorboards and furniture to the rugs and curtains and bedding. It is like being in an institution. It is like a blank canvas. It worries her: she will never manage to keep it nice; sooner or later, she will spoil it.

She would have liked to have the bed by the window, but Sponge has got there first; her suitcase is on the bed, unzipped and spilling its contents. She is standing at the window now, holding her phone as high as she can.

'There's no signal here,' says Sandra, taking her rucksack to the other side of the room.

'I know,' says Sponge, and after a moment she gives up.

In between the two beds is a wide chest of drawers, into which they set about unpacking their belongings. On top, on her side, Sandra places an alarm clock. She won't set it - she will want to wake naturally, not in ragged panic, an alarm interrupting her dreams - but she will want to know the time when she opens her eyes. Other than that, she does not want to be too rigid; she expects it will be quite nice to lose track of time, to allow herself to be guided by the sunrise and the sunset and her appetite, by her own circadian rhythm. She has not even brought her watch.

Next to the clock, she puts the book she has just started, a doorstop of a historical romance. Sponge has a bedside book as well. 'What are you reading?' asks Sandra.

'Angela Carter,' says Sponge, showing her the cover.

'I thought she wrote fairy tales,' says Sandra, looking at the gory title, the ominous artwork. 'That looks like horror.'

'They're not necessarily different things,' says Sponge. 'Take "Bluebeard".'

Sandra is vaguely aware of the story – with the castle and the forbidden room and the dead wives – and would rather not think about it.

'You can borrow it if you like,' says Sponge.

Sandra will not read it; a book like that would give her bad dreams. She read a horror story in her teens and had to sleep with the light on for weeks. She has avoided horror ever since.

Sponge finishes unpacking and heads downstairs, but Sandra wants the bathroom and waits for it to become free. When she hears the bathroom door being unlocked, she goes onto the landing. One of the men is coming out, the baby-faced one. He says to Sandra, 'All settled in? How's your room?'

'It's OK,' says Sandra. 'The view's disappointing. Although Sponge is in the bed by the window anyway.'

'Sponge?' says the man. Sandra feels her face redden, but the man smiles and goes on his way. Sandra goes into the bathroom and closes the door.

She emerges to the sound of somebody downstairs popping a cork. Following the sound of voices down to the hallway, she hears Spiker saying, 'Is she in with you?' A voice that sounds like Sponge's responds indistinctly, and Spiker says, 'She is, isn't she?'

Sandra finds everyone gathered in the lounge, the women sitting together on the three-seater sofa and the men with an armchair each. Spiker, holding an uncorked bottle of wine, is sharing it out between six glasses. The baby-faced man queries this: turning to Sponge, looking pointedly at her so-pregnant belly, he says, 'Are you drinking?'

'Oh yes,' says Sponge, reaching for her glass.

There is a vacant two-seater sofa, on which Sandra sits. 'I don't know who anyone is,' she says, looking around at her housemates. 'Apart from Harriet.'

'I've forgotten your name already,' says Harriet.

'I'm Sandra,' says Sandra. There had been a Harriet at her school, who disliked her, for reasons Sandra never knew.

'That's unusual,' says Sponge, eyeing the wine she's just tasted. 'Is that from the kitchen?'

Spiker takes a sip from her own glass. 'This is what's in the wine rack,' she says. 'It's homemade, elderberry.' She shows Sponge the bottle, the handwritten label. 'There's more in the cellar.'

'I'm a visual artist,' says Sandra. 'I'm going to work on landscapes and seascapes; I want to perfect my watercolour.'

Spiker says, 'I'm Belle.' She goes around the room; she indicates Sponge: 'Angie,' and the men: 'Alan,' who is still in the holiday clothes that seem so unsuited to this climate, and who is now relieving himself of his socks, 'and Colin,' who waves, as if Sandra were a long way away.

Sandra says to Belle, 'And what do you do?'

'I'm multidisciplinary,' says Belle. 'I prefer not to be pigeonholed.'

'I quite agree,' says Alan, putting his socks on the coffee table.

Angie is a poet. 'You can read some of my work if you like,' she says to Sandra, who has no interest whatsoever in poetry.

Colin reaches into the pocket of his combat trousers. He says he collects found objects, and shows them a matchbox.

Angie looks doubtfully at the old matchbox, and Belle says, 'You should try the seashore. I have a friend who collects seashells. She turns them into jewellery.'

Colin slides the matchbox open. Inside is a butterfly, which seems to be dead.

Harriet admires its unusual colours, and Angie says, 'Oh! That's a beauty.'

Perhaps it was, thinks Sandra, but keeping it when it's dead seems grotesque. She asks Colin what he will do with it.

'He doesn't have to do anything with it,' says Belle. 'It's found art.'

'Like Duchamp's urinal,' says Alan.

'But he turned the urinal on its side,' says Angie. 'Otherwise it would just have been a urinal.'

'What about Craig-Martin's glass of water?' says Alan. 'That was just a glass of water.'

'But he *said* it was an oak tree,' says Angie, 'so it was a conceptual work of art.'

'I keep my found objects in a naturalistic setting,' says Colin.

'Like in a museum,' suggests Angie.

'Yes,' says Colin, 'but at home. They're just for me.' He closes the matchbox and puts it away in his pocket.

'Well,' says Sandra, 'it's nice to know who everyone is.' She smiles around at her housemates and says, 'Six is a nice number, isn't it?' She settles back in her seat, thinking *Valerie Swanson probably sat just where I'm sitting.* 'Does anyone know,' she asks, 'which was Valerie Swanson's bedroom? I thought it might be one of the big back rooms.' But no one knows, and no one seems to care very much.

'I'm cooking tonight,' says Belle, standing up. 'We haven't got any fussy eaters, have we?'

Colin shakes his head and Angie says, 'No,' and Harriet says, 'No,' and Alan says, 'I'll eat anything.'

'I'm vegetarian,' says Sandra.

Belle rolls her eyes. She moves through to the kitchen with her glass of wine, saying over her shoulder, 'I'll call you when it's ready.' Sandra takes this as a cue to drift away herself, though the others stay put.

Up in her room, Sandra picks up her novel and lies down on her bed to read, engrossing herself in her romance, in its passions and betrayals. After two chapters, she falls asleep, and is woken from a dream by what sounds like a handbell being rung, like the one they used when she was at school to call the children in from playing. Sitting up, she scrapes her head on the low, sloped ceiling, which makes her feel like Alice in Wonderland grown big, ill-fitting in her strange world. She looks at her clock. She supposes it must be dinnertime: what she can hear is a metal spoon banging about in a pan. Anticipating the cold stone floors downstairs, she is glad of the moccasins that Alex bought her for her fortieth birthday.

Belle is sitting at the head of the table. She is flanked by Angie and Harriet, and next to them are the men. Sandra sits down next to Colin, with an empty chair opposite. *I'm sitting at Valerie Swanson's table*, she thinks. There is more wine on the table, and a tureen. There is a smell of garlic, which does not agree with her, and Stilton, her least favourite cheese.

'That *does* smell good,' says Angie.

Belle has ladled sauce from the tureen onto a plate of pasta which she passes down the table to Sandra, and then ladles sauce onto five plates of steak which the others receive with noises of pleasure and gratitude. Sandra looks warily at her plateful and picks up her fork, then catches Belle's eye and puts it down again.

Belle brings her hands together. 'Father, we thank you,' she says, 'for this wonderful food. We invite your Holy Spirit to be with us as we enjoy this precious time together.' The others say, 'Amen,' and Sandra mouths it, doing her best to fit in.

They start eating, and Colin says, 'This is wonderful, Belle.'

'It's so creamy,' says Angie.

The sauce is far too rich for Sandra. 'Thank you, Belle,' she says. She drinks her wine.

Angie says to Sandra, 'Are you a good cook?'

'I like to cook,' says Sandra.

'But are you any good?' insists Angie. When Sandra hesitates, Angie says, 'Never mind, we'll find out soon enough. We can judge for ourselves, can't we?'

Sandra makes an effort to finish her portion. She is the last to put down her fork. While Harriet clears the table, a two-litre tub of vanilla ice cream is fetched from the chest freezer in the cellar and Belle serves it out. Sandra thinks, as the six of them take up their teaspoons, *It's like being at a children's party.* She reaches for her water glass. It's surprising how different the water tastes here: not unpleasant exactly, but noticeably different. The water is perhaps harder than she is used to, and leaves an aftertaste.

'Thank you, Belle,' says Sandra. 'That was very nice. I'll do the dinner tomorrow.'

Harriet, taking away the dessert bowls, says, 'I'm doing tomorrow.' She rolls up her sleeves.

'The next day, then,' says Sandra.

'Alan's doing the next day,' says Belle.

Sandra wonders when all this was decided.

'I've organised a rota,' says Belle, 'to make sure everyone takes a turn. You're cooking on Monday. You'll have to wash up on Sunday.'

While Harriet is taking care of the first night's washing

up, the rest of the group move through to the lounge, taking their wine glasses with them. Belle takes her place in the middle of the three-seater sofa, with Angie on one side and a space for Harriet on the other. Alan and Colin head for their armchairs, and Sandra takes the two-seater sofa, with enough room to tuck her feet up beside her. Sitting comfortably, she sips at her wine.

'In our house, we have a rule,' says Belle, turning to Sandra. 'No shoes on the sofa.'

'These aren't shoes,' says Sandra. 'These are moccasins.'

'We have the same rule in our house,' says Angie.

'But these are moccasins,' insists Sandra. 'They're slippers, not shoes.'

'Moccasins are shoes,' says Alan.

'I don't think they are,' says Sandra, untucking her feet and putting them flat on the cold floor.

Angie takes out her cigarettes and lights up. Colin watches, looking as if he is on the verge of saying something.

When Harriet comes through to join them, Belle says, 'Now we can play a game.' She decides on a card game that no one knows, and explains the rules as she shuffles the deck and then deals. The game seems to Sandra unnecessarily complicated. Alan asks Harriet if moccasins are shoes, and tells her about Sandra having had them up on the sofa. Harriet finds a dictionary and looks it up. 'Moccasins *are* shoes,' she says, bringing the dictionary to Sandra so that she can read the definition for herself.

'They're not *on* the sofa now anyway,' says Sandra, picking up her hand of cards and fanning them out.

Belle goes first, taking a card from the stack and discarding one from her hand. 'I play this with my children,' she says.

Angie takes her turn, lifting a card from the stack and

placing another on the discard pile, and asks how old they are.

'Fourteen and fifteen, nearly sixteen,' says Belle. 'They won't be children much longer.'

'Same with mine,' says Harriet. 'But I don't suppose we'd be here otherwise. You don't want to leave them when they're little, do you?'

Sandra studies her cards. She has not quite grasped the rules of this game.

Colin takes his turn, selecting a card and discarding a card, and then it is Sandra's go. She takes a card from the stack, adds it to her hand, and puts one down on the discard pile. Alan picks it up. As they go around the circle, Sandra gets into the rhythm, picking up and discarding, collecting some pairs and some runs, picking up and discarding . . .

'You don't want to do that,' says Belle, looking down at the card Sandra's just discarded.

Sandra looks at her. Alan picks the card up and says to Sandra, 'You're out.'

'I'm out?' says Sandra. 'How come?' But she does not pay much attention to the explanation. She does not like this game anyway. She puts down her cards, not caring that she is out, not caring that she does not understand why. Harriet takes her turn and Sandra sits back, yawning. Her feet, through the soles of her moccasins, have grown cold against the stone tiles. She wonders if she wants another drink, and decides she wants her bed. 'I know it's still early,' she says, standing up, 'but I'm going to have to go to bed.' She rubs her eyes and moves towards the door.

'All right,' says Belle, considering her cards.

'Night night,' says Sandra.

She climbs the stairs. Down in the hallway, Alan is on his way into the kitchen, saying, 'I'll fetch us another bottle of wine.' Sandra could not have faced another glass anyway. She regrets cleaning her plate, and then having dessert. She feels horribly heavy. First thing in the morning, she will run.

5

IT WAS DURING one of Carol's early novel-writing attempts - when she was in theory writing a first draft of a
first chapter but was in fact online, going down some rabbit
hole - that she received an email from some film students.
They made flattering remarks about her work, and about one
short story in particular, which was one of her darkest. They
were interested, they said, in making it into a short film for
their final-year project, and Carol gave them permission.

The students were very sweet, and got in touch from time
to time with updates. Through the university, they had access
to the equipment they needed, and they had some private
funding, local sponsors, and they had the perfect location:
they knew someone who knew someone who owned a big
house on a little island. And that was Roman.

Carol had understood that the students had arranged to
shoot the whole film on the island, sleeping in the house,
which had running water and electricity and so on - but
something had not worked out, although Carol is not clear
what that something was. A disagreement, she assumed, although Roman has said not. Anyway, the students cut the
trip short and left the island having filmed only the exterior
scenes. They went back to the mainland, where the team fell
apart. Carol assumed that the project had been abandoned,
and she had almost forgotten about the whole thing when, out
of the blue, she received the finished film. The interior scenes

had been shot in a different house, on the mainland, the two locations seamlessly edited together. Carol watched the film on her laptop. For an undergraduate project, she thought it was rather good, if shaky in places.

It was at that point, via the students, that Carol actually met Roman. He asked what she was working on now and she told him about her fantasy novel, though she had still written next to nothing, or nothing worth keeping. 'What I need,' she said, 'is no distractions, then I expect I'd get it done,' and then he offered her his little island, his empty house.

'Although,' he said, 'I doubt you would want it. It's terribly isolated, and dreadfully neglected, I'm afraid. It's what you might call *atmospheric*. And while the house is not entirely without modern conveniences, it would be a far cry from what you're used to.'

'That wouldn't bother me,' she told him.

Well, he said, she was welcome to it, and she would be doing him a favour, being there, keeping an eye on the place, just until he could sell it.

'I wouldn't want to stay there,' says Jayne, when Carol tells her about this conversation. Jayne has seen the film, which, she said, gave her the willies. 'That house is creepy as fuck.'

'I wouldn't put it quite like that,' says Carol, who dislikes bad language. Her mother was very strict about such things, and Carol was the same with her son. *I won't have it in my house.* 'It's *supposed* to look creepy in the film,' she tells Jayne. 'It's all lighting and editing.'

'It's in the middle of nowhere,' says Jayne. She fills their glasses, emptying the bottle.

'It's just so I can write this novel,' says Carol. Although, of course, if she wants to write a series, when she finally finishes this novel she must write another one. Perhaps the house will never sell; perhaps she will never come back.

'When are you going?' asks Jayne.

'This weekend,' says Carol.

'So soon?' says Jayne. She shakes her head, and flags down a waiter, wanting the dessert menu and another bottle of wine. 'We should indulge,' she says to Carol, 'while we still can.'

6

SANDRA SETS OFF at sunrise, wearing old brown leggings and a baggy green sweatshirt. She used to do cross-country running at school, on occasional weekends. She always seemed to be at the back. When she turned forty, it struck her that one of these days she would try to run a mile or half a mile and find that she could not, so now she is trying to run, to be a runner, before it's too late. She has read that running is beneficial for people over the age of forty; she has also read that it might be detrimental, but she will keep doing it. It feels like a good thing to do, and she has started to crave it, along with the runner's high that she has heard so much about. She will keep going until she is forced – by Achilles tendonitis or runner's knee or whatever else – to stop.

She runs in the direction of the dock. It is bitingly cold out; the island smells so fresh. She has her Walkman, and a compilation designed to push her on, to make her move faster. With her head full of music, she cannot hear her own feet pounding the dirt track.

The rising sun casts her shadow onto the hedge to her left. The sky is almost cloudless and her shadow stays with her until it is swallowed up by the dense woodland. It occurs to her that this outfit she is wearing, which is fine on the pavements in the suburbs, where she has always been quite safe, is not ideal in the countryside: if she stood still, she could pass for a tree, she would just blend in. At least she is wearing her gloves, bright pink gloves that will make her more visible. There is still the danger, of course, of something coming up behind her unseen and unheard, and of being oblivious until it is almost upon her.

When the track reaches the dock, it comes to an abrupt stop. At some point, she will sit here and paint Liel, the blur of it on the horizon, and the ten miles of sea in between.

There are no boats in sight. The ferry will not come today; it comes and goes on Wednesdays. Besides, at this hour, the jetty is submerged.

She turns around and runs back the way she came. She doubts she has gone even half a mile before she is back at the house. She was planning to run on but is in danger of missing breakfast: through the kitchen window, she can see Alan filling a mug from the coffee pot, and Harriet carrying a plate, beckoning her in. Anyway, she thinks, it might be better not to go too far on this uneven track and get an injury on the very first day.

She heads inside, but by the time she has taken her trainers off and put her Walkman away, the kitchen is deserted. She makes herself some toast, and eats it at the table while the kettle boils. She is spooning the tea bag out of her mug when Angie comes in.

'Have you just made a cup for yourself?' asks Angie.

'Yes,' says Sandra, still balancing the tea bag on the spoon.

'We've been using the tea pot,' explains Angie. 'So that there's enough for everyone.'

'Oh,' says Sandra. 'I hadn't realised.'

Angie refills the kettle and says, 'I expect you're an only child, are you?'

'No,' says Sandra defensively, although she is.

Angie makes a pot of tea. 'We're all in the garden,' she says. 'Are you coming out?'

Sandra goes over to the kitchen window and peers along the patio. She can see them now, all gathered around a picnic table. 'I'm going to take my tea upstairs and have a shower,' she says.

'Suit yourself,' says Angie, and goes to join the others.

Undressing in the chilly bathroom gives Sandra goose pimples. She waits for the water to run warm, before realising that it is only getting cooler, that the last of the hot is running out. She gets in beneath the lukewarm spray and pulls the flimsy curtain across.

When shopping for skincare products, she has started to look at cleansers and serums and moisturisers that promise to brighten and rejuvenate, to firm and refine, and she does want that but they are prohibitively expensive. Sometimes, she acquires a free sample, a single sachet or a tiny tube from a luxury brand, which runs out before she can see if it really works. Perhaps she should just stick to her budget basics, but these samples of things that are out of her price range are so tempting.

After showering, she puts on the set of old clothes she's brought for painting in and heads downstairs with the canvas satchel in which she keeps her art materials. The men are on their way out, with rucksacks on their backs. Belle and Harriet are in the hallway, zipping up their coats. Angie is sitting at the bottom of the stairs, lacing her boots. Sandra squeezes past her and goes into the kitchen, where she makes herself a packed lunch, an egg sandwich, and when she comes out, they've all gone. The retreat, she thinks, is not what she expected. On the other hand, when she dwells on this, what she expected seems vague. But it wasn't this.

She heads out, helping herself to an apple from one of the trees as she goes by. There is no one in sight, in any direction; she could imagine herself alone here, with this retreat all to herself, Valerie Swanson's house all to herself. She turns right, away from the part of the island she has already seen. She has no plan, but she does not expect to go too far wrong on an island of this size.

It is a glorious day: sharp and bright. With gorse on one side and brambles on the other, she might have been on a country lane not far from home. After a hundred yards or so, a narrower path branches off to the right of the main track, and Sandra takes it. The landscape is a collage of secondary colours, her path cutting through sea-green grass and gingery bracken and heather the colour of her fleece, and bringing her to the shore. Beyond her feet, the path crumbles onto the sand.

She walks along a little way, this side of the eroding edge, the coarse grass stabbing her ankles, until she finds a lone rock, the right size for a perch and invitingly smooth. She sits down and looks out at the seascape. Today, the sea is more grey than green.

She wonders if, even now, it is too late for her to go to art college. But she has a fear that she will find she does not have the talent for it after all, or the motivation, the passion, or something. Her godfather was an artist, and moderately successful. But his creative experience seemed to consist of long periods of slogging, or blockage, and maddening frustration, in pursuit of brief orgasmic moments of insight or creative breakthrough which Sandra has never had and can hardly imagine but which he seemed to live for and which she wants. In midlife, and mid-painting, he walked out of his flat and disappeared.

Sandra unpacks her satchel. She fills her water pot from her water bottle and opens her paint set. When she opened the tin for the first time, when it was brand-new, she thought it looked so beautiful: all those little blocks of pigment, all the colours of the rainbow and then some, not yet used. Now, it's a bit of a mess. She sharpens her pencil. Some people don't use a pencil but she would feel totally lost without at least a faint line to guide her. She opens her watercolour pad, loving the look of the clean, unspoiled page. She secures the corners with bulldog clips. She has lost enough work to the wind.

She takes a deep breath.

She draws a steady pencil line across the middle of the page, feeling like a surgeon sliding a scalpel across a taut belly, hoping not to be surprised by a sneeze. She looks at her line, then rubs it out, then draws it in again in the same place as before. She wets her brush, then wets the page above the line. All right. She approaches the colours, selecting the ultramarine, which is her favourite of them all. She has to water it right down though, and paints it onto the page with a waterlogged brush. She has been warned about this: she uses too much water; she drowns her brush. She must be more careful.

She sits and waits for her sky to dry out, and mixes the grey for her sea.

Her sea looks like stone, like concrete. She would have liked to put boats on the water, but there are none, and anyway, on this car-park-coloured sea they would look as if they had run aground. Her sky is dry now, but it has faded; it is frustratingly pale. She would have liked to put birds in it, but although she can hear the gulls she cannot see them;

there's an incongruous magpie, which is not what she wants.

Her failure is causing an unpleasant restlessness in her stomach, or perhaps she's just hungry. She sets the picture aside, hoping that when she looks at it again she will like it better.

She unwraps her egg sandwich and eats it slowly, watching the unbroken horizon. She eats her apple, even though it is tart. When she has packed her lunch away, she looks at her picture again, and likes it no better than before. She is annoyed by her bad start but is determined to improve. That's enough for one day though.

She rinses her brushes and dries them on a rag, pours away her water and removes the bulldog clips from her pad. She puts everything back in her satchel and stands up, aching from sitting on the stone. She feels like a bird that has spent hours sitting on an egg that has not hatched.

She walks a little further along the coastline, picking wild flowers as she goes. Some she recognises, or thinks she does; some she does not know. Some are pretty and delicate; some are frankly ugly, though she finds these more interesting. When she has a collection, she sits down and sets about trying to sketch them, one per page, in a scrapbook. Later, she will press the flowers and then she will tape each one onto the page beside its sketch, which will serve as a reminder of what she was aiming for versus what she achieved.

By the time Sandra returns to the house, the hallway is full of boots and coats and the smell of cooking coming from the kitchen and the sound of voices coming from the lounge. She takes off her outdoor things and climbs the stairs.

In her bedroom, she sets about pressing her wild flowers, flattening them with the weight of her historical romance.

Then she changes out of her work clothes and into something nice: a long, floral, chiffon dress that she finds flattering, and an ornate silver necklace that Alex gave her. She makes her way downstairs.

Everyone else is in the kitchen now, though Sandra did not hear anyone calling her down. Harriet has been busy cooking an impressive roast chicken dinner: there are five full, steaming plates on the table, and a cheese salad in Sandra's place.

Belle, eyeing Sandra's outfit, says, 'Are you going somewhere nice?'

'Oh,' says Sandra. 'No.' She looks around at the others, none of whom has changed. She feels too smart now, too formal for the occasion.

'She's joking,' says Colin. 'Where could you go?'

Harriet leads grace. Sandra does not say 'amen' and Alan looks at her but says nothing.

'I missed my own cooker,' says Harriet, picking up her knife and fork. 'I'm used to gas.'

'I miss my wine cellar,' says Alan, reaching for the home-made wine. 'This stuff's drinkable but there's not much choice.'

'I miss my hot tub,' says Belle. 'We could do with a hot tub here, on the patio, don't you think?' There is a chorus of agreement. 'I want a soak in a hot tub and two fingers of single malt whisky.'

'I can't stand the smell of whisky,' says Sandra.

'I'm missing my book group tonight,' says Angie. 'We're reading Angela Carter. Some of it's quite good.'

'I'm going to miss my potholing,' says Colin. 'A group of us go once a week.'

'That's very adventurous of you,' says Harriet.

'I don't think I could do it,' says Belle.

'I wouldn't want to do it,' agrees Sandra. She doesn't even

like to imagine it: venturing into an unknown cave system, moving systematically forward into a narrowing space, and suddenly – no doubt having made an error of judgement, perhaps falling or getting caught out by flooding, finding that she can go no further, and that she cannot turn back – finding herself stuck, with no choice but to wait for the air to run out. 'Being trapped would be my greatest fear,' she says.

'What will you miss, Sandra?' asks Belle.

'All sorts of things, I expect,' says Sandra. 'But I've wanted to come to Lieloh for as long as I can remember. I can hardly believe I'm actually here.'

'Is it living up to your expectations?' asks Angie.

'It's been a bit of a disappointing day to be honest,' says Sandra.

'Oh well,' says Angie.

Sandra is the last to finish eating. She does not think of herself as a slow eater, but apparently she is. The moment she puts her knife and fork together, Alan clears the table.

Harriet dishes out the vanilla ice cream, and Sandra eats quickly so as not to be last again and gives herself an ice-cream headache. When Alan begins gathering the empty bowls on his side of the table, Sandra sets about collecting together the bowls on her side. 'No,' says Harriet, moving her dish out of Sandra's reach. 'It's Alan's turn.'

While Alan washes up, the remaining five go through to the lounge. They take their seats, except for Colin, who is interested in the record player. Discovering a lone record, he reads the name of the artist from the sleeve: 'Josephine Baker. Has anyone heard of Josephine Baker?' Nobody has. He places the record on the turntable, sets it spinning and lifts the needle over, and there is Josephine Baker singing 'Then I'll Be Happy'. The old, jazzy music raises a few smiles. When Alan comes in, Colin says, 'Listen to this.' He plays it again, and Alan responds with a little dance, receiving applause, before sitting down in his armchair and taking off his socks.

Belle suggests a sharing of work and asks for volunteers.

'I've been working on a new poem,' says Angie. 'I don't know if it's any good.'

'We'd love to hear it,' says Belle.

'I have some sketches I could show,' says Harriet.

'Wonderful,' says Belle. 'What about you, Sandra? What have you been doing with yourself today?'

'I had a go at a painting this morning,' says Sandra.

'Well go and fetch it then,' says Belle.

Sandra bristles at Belle's self-imposed authority, but goes to fetch her bad painting from her room. She sits for a minute on the edge of her bed, considering it. She is not at all happy with it. It lacks life. The best she can say about it is that she has stayed within the lines. But, she tells herself, this is what she has come here for; she must be brave. She carries her work downstairs and says, as she enters the lounge, 'I don't think—'

'Ssh . . .' says Belle.

'The stone,' says Angie, 'turning cold.'

'That was beautiful,' says Harriet.

'Thank you,' says Angie. She closes her notebook.

'Yes,' says Belle. 'Absolutely beautiful.' The room murmurs and nods its approval. 'Well done.'

'Thank you,' says Angie.

Sandra, sitting on the smaller sofa with her bad painting on her knees, says, 'I loved the final line.'

'We did wait,' says Belle, 'but then we started without you.'

'This is the painting I did today,' says Sandra, turning it towards the others. 'I don't think it's very good. There's room for improvement.'

42

'There's always room for improvement,' says Belle, 'and that's what we're here for, isn't it?'

Sandra is flagging. When Angie accepts another glass of wine and Colin suggests she has perhaps had enough and Angie responds by fetching another bottle, Sandra goes up to bed.

That was just the first day, she thinks, as she brushes her teeth. There is always tomorrow.

Angie's cigarette smoke has drifted upstairs and is trapped in the bedroom. Sandra opens the window. It might be a cold night but she will want fresh air while she sleeps. She changes into her nightie and puts her evening dress on its hanger on the back of the door. She is in bed and almost asleep when Angie comes in and, complaining about the cold, closes the window.

'I'd like the window open,' says Sandra.

'But I want it closed,' says Angie, 'and I was here first.'

'I was here first,' says Sandra.

'I was here first when we chose our beds,' says Angie. 'I got the bed by the window, and I want the window closed.'

Angie sits up reading her book of fairy tales or horror stories or whatever they are, the light keeping Sandra awake until eventually she gives up trying to sleep. Turning to Angie, she asks, 'What was your poem about?'

'The chapel,' says Angie.

'The chapel?' says Sandra.

'I mentioned it earlier,' says Angie.

'I don't think I was there,' says Sandra.

'You were there,' says Angie. 'Belle's right, you're in a world of your own.'

I *wish*, thinks Sandra. At least then she'd be in charge of the windows.

'The Swanson family chapel,' says Angie. 'It's at the far end of the island.'

'I had no idea there even was a Swanson family chapel,' says Sandra.

'Well,' says Angie, 'it's there.'

Even an island as small as Lieloh could spring a few surprises.

'I wrote the poem for my husband,' says Angie.

'I'm sure he'll love it,' says Sandra.

'He's dead,' says Angie.

'I'm so sorry,' says Sandra. 'I didn't know.'

'The others knew,' says Angie. 'It's the first thing I've written since he died.'

'Well,' says Sandra, who has started her sentence without knowing how it might end, and is still groping for words when Angie puts aside her book and turns out the light.

7

EARLY ON THE morning of Carol's flight, Jayne drives
her friend to the airport. For a while, they are travelling
in darkness, listening to odd radio programmes they are not
normally up in time to hear. By the time the sun comes up,
they can see signs to Carol's terminal. Jayne heads for the
short-stay car park. 'If you let me know when you're coming
back,' she says as she parks, 'I'll come and pick you up.'

Jayne wheels Carol's big suitcase towards the departure
hall while Carol carries her hand luggage. 'I wish you weren't
going,' says Jayne.

'It won't be for ever,' says Carol.

'You'll be miserable,' says Jayne, 'without your dresses, and
your nice shoes.'

'I won't need them,' says Carol. 'I'll wear jeans and jumpers,
or nothing at all if I feel like it, and no make-up, and no one
will be there to see me.' She might be a city girl at heart, but
she is really looking forward to breathing clean air, unpol-
luted air. She is imagining her stay being like the country
breaks she sometimes goes on, when she might do some
walking but also gets to spend hours and hours lounging
about reading books in the seclusion of her hotel room, so it
will be like that, except that those hours and hours are to be
spent writing, and instead of a quick weekend she will be there
indefinitely.

Inside the departure hall, they look at the information

on the overhead monitors and eye the desks, the queues, and Carol fishes her ticket out of her bag.

'Call me,' says Jayne. 'You *will* be able to call me, won't you?'

'Not from my mobile,' says Carol, 'there's no signal, but there's a landline.'

'And I'll write,' says Jayne. 'If I write you a letter, will it reach you?'

'I think the ferryman will bring it,' says Carol.

'All right then,' says Jayne.

They say goodbye, and they hug, and then Carol says, 'I'd better go or I'll miss my flight.'

'Yes,' says Jayne.

'Wish me luck!' says Carol.

'Good luck,' says Jayne.

Carol makes her way towards the check-in desk, turning once to wave to Jayne, who is still watching her go.

By the time Jayne is home and lunching alone, Carol will be on Liel; she will be at the docks, wheeling her suitcase down the ramp to the ferry that is waiting to take her across to Roman's island, which will be like her own little island, at least for now.

8

THE BEDROOM'S WHITE curtains are terrible at keeping out the daylight, which wakes Sandra when she would have preferred to stay sleeping. But it is, she sees, high time she got up; it will do no good lying around as if she has all the time in the world. She must get going; she must get to work on her art. She sits up, bumping her head on the sloped ceiling. Her cursing wakes Angie, who sees Sandra moving about and says, 'Are you going to run?'

'Not today,' says Sandra. It can do more harm than good, she understands, to run every day. Yesterday's run was so short, though, that she expects it hardly counts.

The bathroom is occupied so Sandra goes downstairs in her nightie and moccasins. She feels like an overgrown child on a sleepover in a strange house, like she ought to be clutching her teddy.

Others are already up and eating breakfast in the garden – she can see them through the window, sitting at the picnic table on the patio. She makes some toast and a mug of tea and heads outside. She hears someone saying, '. . . very strange woman.' They are quiet as she approaches and sits down.

'We were just talking about Valerie Swanson,' says Belle.

'Oh,' says Sandra. 'The elusive Valerie Swanson.' She looked her up in the library, in an encyclopedia of film stars, but her entry was tiny. There was a still of her, though, from the twenties, posed in silent horror at the looming of some villain.

When Sandra thinks of Valerie Swanson now, this is what she is picturing, just as Harold Lloyd will be forever hanging from that clock, clinging to the minute hand, dangling far above the city, his legs flailing in mid-air. She used to watch Harold Lloyd on television. There was something fascinating about that soundless drama, the silent peril – not that the films were truly silent of course: there was the jazzy music, which Sandra did not care for; she preferred them muted. She watched Charlie Chaplin too, and Laurel and Hardy, and other big names from that era, but Valerie Swanson was not among them. 'I don't really know much about her.'

'There's a book all about her in the lounge,' says Angie.

'She was up-and-coming in the silent era,' says Belle, 'but then talkies came in and that was the end of that.'

'Plenty of people transitioned from silents to talkies,' says Sandra. As well as all those old faces she knew from television, she mentions Greta Garbo, Joan Crawford, Carole Lombard . . .

'But Valerie Swanson's voice was wrong,' says Belle.

'She had a really awful voice,' agrees Angie.

'She retired before she was twenty,' says Belle. 'I doubt she was greatly missed. Apparently she was a nightmare to work with. Her biography is rather unflattering.'

'What did she do,' asks Sandra, 'after retiring from the film industry?'

'I don't think she did anything much,' says Belle. 'She had her house built and barely left it. She was quite self-sufficient. She grew her own fruit – our elderberry wine seems to be an old family recipe – and vegetables. Apparently, she used wild garlic in almost everything, raw as well, and reeked of the stuff; you would know just from the smell that she was there.' She shrugs. 'She spent most of her life as a recluse.'

Sandra has never thought of Valerie Swanson as a recluse,

48

but of course – she lived alone on a private island. In Sandra's mind's eye, Valerie gains a wilder look: her hair grows unwashed and wind-tangled, her silk gown turns shabby.

'But she threw incredible parties,' says Sandra.

'Did she?' says Belle.

'Apparently,' says Sandra.

Belle, looking unconvinced, gathers up her crockery. The others are leaving the table, going inside, but Sandra hasn't finished. She remains alone, eating her toast and drinking her tea and considering the house. It must, then, have been built around 1930, but it seems older than that, presumably due to neglect.

She looks around the garden. She dreamt about a garden last night, though not this one. The garden in her dream was glorious and full of life; it was vast and supremely peaceful. It was no garden she has ever known.

Sandra returns her plate and mug to the kitchen, then takes another cool shower.

Wearing her painting clothes, carrying her satchel, ready to try again, she goes downstairs and, while everyone else is leaving the house, makes another egg sandwich. There are plenty of those tart apples growing on the trees, so she picks a couple and puts them in her bag.

She walks in the same direction as the previous day. Where the narrower path branches off to the right, she follows it, returning to the same shore. Sitting on the stone egg, she opens up her satchel and gets out the seascape with which she was so disappointed. Looking at it again in the cold morning light, she is still disappointed. She takes out her watercolours and works on it until it is irretrievable, and then she tears it up and starts again.

'There's a whole island to explore!' says Belle.

Sandra jumps. The tip of her brush grazes the page like a needle skidding over a record. She did not hear anyone approaching, but there is Belle, standing over her, looking over her shoulder at the work in progress, saying, 'You can't sit in the same spot every day.'

'It's only the second day,' says Sandra. 'I'm still working on the same view.'

'You mustn't restrict yourself,' says Belle. 'Creativity is fluid, it needs movement.'

She is already walking on, along the coastline, and Sandra is forced to shout after her, 'Should I walk and paint at the same time?' Belle does not respond. It was supposed to sound sarcastic but it sounds like a genuine question, rather desperate and shrill.

Sandra returns to her work. Her idea of what she wants is very clear, yet when she stops and looks at the view in front of her and then at what she has on the page, it is not what she wanted at all. The whole thing is wrong; it is too flat, too bare.

She considers the problem while unwrapping her sandwich. She can no more get this seascape onto the page than she could the breeze or the temperature or the smell of the grass and salt water. Between one glance and the next, something moves, everything changes. And she does not know when to stop, to say to herself not so much *I have had my vision* but *That will have to do*. She wants something more tangible, just there on the horizon.

She looks down at her lap and sees that she has eaten her sandwich. She puts away the wrapper and wipes her mouth, then picks up her pad and her brush. She paints in the sun that has, all this time, been creeping over the sky towards her, and adds a boat that is not there, but none of it looks real.

She is uncomfortable on her stone egg. It is only when she stands up, cramped and sore, that she realises she has been sitting on the wrong rock; this rock is smaller than the first, and not as smooth.

Sandra closes the front door behind her and stoops to unlace her boots. She can hear the murmur of people gathered in the lounge, and, as she hangs up her coat, Josephine Baker. She climbs the stairs, quiet in her socks.

She puts away her satchel and strips off her painting clothes. It has been a frustrating day and she is glad to get out of them. She puts on her dress, which she packed thinking it would be perfect for the evenings. She sees, now, how out of place it is. She could wear her travelling outfit – the clothes she arrived in, the clothes she would wear to go home – but she prefers her special dress. She found it in a vintage shop and wore it on her first anniversary with Alex. They had champagne cocktails, and Alex had oysters; there was a red rose and a serenade. 'Imagine,' she said to Alex, 'if we lived like this all the time.' In the novels she enjoys, there are big houses, and extensive gardens to stroll in, and a heroine who – when the gong sounds – sweeps down the staircase in a gown into which she has changed just for dinner.

She can hear the spoon banging on the saucepan, and makes her way down.

'Here she comes,' says Belle, eyeing Sandra's floor-length dress, her jewellery. 'The lady of the manor.'

'The clothes I had on have got paint on them,' says Sandra.

'You should try pencil,' says Harriet. 'I use pencil. It's less messy.'

'I have tried pencil,' says Sandra. 'I had an exhibition that included some portraits done in pencil.' The exhibition, in a local gallery, had been arranged through one of Sandra's evening classes. There had been a grand opening, a private view; people, dressed up, holding glasses of wine, paused in front of her pictures, before moving on. 'But I don't really have a knack for people.' Belle and Harriet exchange a look that Sandra can't decipher. 'I prefer paint,' she adds.

After grace, Alan cuts into the quiche he has made. 'It would have been bigger,' he says, 'but there weren't enough eggs. I suspect someone's been eating them.'

'I've been having them in my sandwiches,' says Sandra.

'That'll be it then,' says Alan.

'It doesn't matter, Alan,' says Angie. 'I'm sure there's still plenty to go around.'

He divides the quiche into five pieces and passes them along to everyone except Sandra, for whom he has made a cheese salad.

'It's a salmon quiche,' he says. 'It's my mother's recipe, but it's never quite the same.'

Colin, tasting it, says it's very nice and asks for the recipe, and Alan says he'll write it down for him. 'Although,' adds Colin, 'my wife is eating nothing but mashed potato. She's suffering from morning sickness.' Sandra remembers keenly that first trimester of pregnancy and the sickness that was not morning sickness but round-the-clock sickness; it felt like constant travel sickness, even though she hardly left the house.

'Well, congratulations,' says Angie, raising a toast to Colin, who shakes his head.

'It's not mine,' he says. 'We're not keeping it. She's a surrogate.'

He takes a sip of his wine, and picks at his small piece of quiche.

After their vanilla ice cream, they take their drinks into the lounge. Sandra puts her wine glass down next to the *History of Art* book. This, she supposes, is something she ought to be reading. She lifts the cover and turns the large pages. The text is tiny and the book is a good two inches thick. It would take her for ever to get through these thousands and thousands of years.

She is always pleased by cave art, by the thought of prehistoric humans wanting to paint a decent horse, a lifelike bison. She flips through Egyptian art and Greek art. She spends a long time looking at a pair of Roman vistas: a city and a garden, each one painted on a wall. They are promised lands, insists the text, that cannot be entered.

Then the Renaissance, followed by *The Ecstasy of St. Theresa*, in which the subject is captured in great pain, in marble.

Sandra studies a page of still lifes, whose objects might carry a message, though not a message she understands. It's like looking at Tarot cards: you have to know the meaning. The Hanged Man can just mean feeling trapped. She casts her eye over a smashed glass, an upturned dish, an abandoned lemon, but needs the text to tell her that this still life implies an unexpected departure, and another one advocates self-restraint.

She quite likes Constable, and Turner. Here is van Gogh, poor man. Towards the end of his life, he moved to Arles, wanting to found an artists' colony but instead entering a series of asylums, dying from a self-inflicted wound, and still young.

Expressionism, abstraction, fantasy . . . No, not her sort of thing.

Colin finishes the washing up and joins them in the lounge. He is already humming 'Then I'll Be Happy' as he makes his way over to the record player and sets it going. Meanwhile, Alan has been looking in the games cupboard. He comes away with Battleship and challenges Colin to a game.

'Battleship!' says Sandra. 'I used to play that.' She remembers winning as well, at least once.

Alan, noting her enthusiasm, says, 'It's a two-player game.'

Angie hunts out a Monopoly set. Sandra has never liked Monopoly. She finds it interminable. She says as much while Angie is setting it up.

'You don't have to play,' says Angie.

'No, I'll play,' says Sandra.

'Don't start if you're going to quit halfway through,' says Belle.

'I'll play,' says Sandra. 'I'll be the boot.'

'I'm the boot,' says Angie.

Sandra looks at the pieces.

'I'm the car,' says Belle.

In the end, Sandra is the dog. She plays for more than an hour, while the men sink their ships and start again, and then sits back. The room is thick with Angie's cigarette smoke. Sandra can feel it clogging her lungs. 'I've had enough,' she says. 'I'm going to go to bed.'

'But we haven't finished the game,' says Angie.

'You can have my properties,' says Sandra, pushing her cards towards Angie.

'You can't do that,' says Belle.

But Sandra is already up on her feet; she is already walking away. She closes the lounge door behind her so that she cannot hear them bitching about her as she climbs the stairs.

She remembers going to a sleepover in her teens, along with that girl Harriet, the school friend who disliked her. Sandra had been so excited about going, wearing her best nightie as if it were a party dress. There were makeovers: they put on glittery make-up, which did not suit Sandra at all. There were bunk beds and camp beds and sleeping bags on the floor, and there was a midnight feast. The chattering and teasing continued even after the parents had been in, even after lights out. All the feast food was finished and Harriet was being mean and Sandra was pretending to sleep. She could hear the other girls giggling, and kept her eyes shut, just wanting the party to be over.

9

CAROL IS THE little ferry's only passenger. When they have put some miles behind them, and with miles still to go, she tries to make small-talk with the ferryman, but he is unforthcoming. He is hunched into his old khaki anorak, furrowing his brow beneath his steel-grey hair, which is close-cropped like a helmet.

The ferryman will come once a week to deliver groceries and anything else Carol might need to make it through the coming months. He will bring her mail, and take away the waste. The arrangement was made through Roman. It is only now – seeing how apathetically the ferryman delivers her to the island, how displeased he seems unloading her luggage, how dourly he tells her, 'Take care,' and how quickly he leaves – that Carol gets the impression that he would rather not come here at all, and perhaps regrets having agreed even to this initial journey.

Hooking a bag over her shoulder and taking the handle of her big suitcase-on-wheels, Carol moves her luggage from the jetty onto the shore of the island.

In between the jetty and a path leading up to the house is a pair of palm trees between which she must pass. They lean together, forming an arch, reminding her of the metal detectors at the airport that forced her to empty her pockets, to remove her phone, her valuables. Half expecting the palm trees to object to her, she passes through.

The big suitcase is having difficulty on the little path. Its wheels do not like the rough terrain. Further along, overgrown privet shrubs intrude on either side, which doesn't help.

Roman has told her to keep an eye out for green lizards and grass snakes, and, he said, there had been talk of a red-backed shrike in the vicinity, though he had not seen it himself. Carol said she wouldn't recognise one if it was standing in front of her, so Roman searched on his phone and showed her a striking little bird with a strip of black across its eyes like a bandit's mask, like a highway robber. *The red-backed shrike*, said the text beneath the image, *is a lovely mini-predator, known as the 'butcher bird', as it impales its prey on thorn bushes.* 'They were thought to have disappeared,' said Roman, 'but now apparently they're back.' *A creature we thought we had lost but found to be still among us*, said the text, *like Lazarus*.

There will be bedding and towels waiting for her inside the house, even toiletries, and a fully stocked kitchen: Roman has seen to all that. Even though this feels, so far, like a holiday, Carol is determined to get down to work as soon as possible, to get this novel written before her deadline's up, before the place is sold, then she'll go home. The ferryman will take her back to Liel, and the aeroplane will return her to the mainland, and Jayne will meet her at the airport, and they'll go somewhere nice for lunch.

It is strange to see the house in the flesh, as it were, having seen the students' film, which drew on the uncanny, uneasy, unsettling quality of her short story, though the way it was done, it was, in the end, more like horror than fantasy. She is pleased to see that the house has been freshly painted: it is bright white, with a glossy sea-green door, and doesn't look creepy at all.

Roman has provided her with a key, which is big and

brassy like a stage prop, like a key to a castle or a magic kingdom. When she opens the door, a part of her expects – despite knowing that there had been this splicing of locations – to find herself in the world of the film. Instead, she enters a very different house, whose wide hallway is filled with sunlight coming in through the open door. A colourful carpet starts at the threshold and snakes up the grand staircase ahead of her. *It's not creepy,* she insists to herself, and she brings in her luggage and closes the door.

10

SANDRA LEAVES THE house with a cheese sandwich in her satchel and her fleece under her coat to keep out the cold. Some of the others have coats that look like duvets; they are well protected. Sandra is wearing her walking coat, her most practical coat, but it is insufficient.

She strolls along the dirt track, between the gorse and the brambles. She passes the turn-off to the right, pressing on along the main track. Aloe vera is growing here, and bamboo, and something else whose name she doesn't know. After another hundred yards, she reaches a second turn-off, a path leading off to the left. She follows it through the grassland and comes to the sea. Lieloh is so small, she cannot go far in any direction without reaching the edge.

She goes down onto the stony beach. To the north, a perfect tumble of boulders extends into the sea, like a sculpture, like found art. It forms a natural wall, so Sandra walks south, along the shore, stopping every now and again to pick up a pebble, putting the prettier stones into her satchel, tossing the other ones into the sea, until the idea that this will only make the island incrementally smaller makes her feel uneasy and she stops.

She finds a spot in which to sit and unpacks her art materials. With her pad on her lap, she considers the view, which is almost identical to the one she painted, rather badly, the day before, except for this slowly rising sun searing the horizon, and a bluer sea, which looks less cold than yesterday's, although presumably it would not be. She makes her pencil marks, and wets her brush.

She remembers a glorious sunrise, honeymooning with Alex. They had got up early, wrapped up warm and walked in the dawn light to the viewing point to wait. And it had been worth it, to see the sun being birthed into the sky, staining the clouds pink. It is one of her happiest memories. She wishes she could have painted it, but she would have needed the sun to stay still. She did take a photograph, in which the sun looked too small.

She is working on her clouds – which are wispy and evasive, drifting and dispersing before her eyes – when she becomes aware of a voice somewhere behind her. 'I mean,' says the voice, 'she doesn't even *try* to fit in.' Another voice murmurs a reply. Sandra refrains from turning around, but she cannot help seeing, out of the corner of her eye, a flash of apricot.

Irked by the interruption, she pauses, assessing her progress. The blue of her sky is bleeding into the blue of her sea, which is still too flat on the page. She has lost the horizon that she so carefully pencilled in. Her frothy waves look more like clouds than her clouds. She turns the picture upside down; it could work either way, were it not for the sun, which looks somehow cold and out of place, like a yellow moon. She tries to make it warmer, adding orange, and then stops, unhappy with the apricot blob that now dominates the picture. She paints in a gull. Her watercolour teacher forbade the use of white – it was, she said, off-limits – but it is right there in Sandra's set and she just wants to use a little bit. She finds the bird tricky though; she is heavy-handed, and regrets her attempt. She does not even like gulls, which do not come hoping for crumbs as garden birds do; they just take whatever you've got, snatch it right out of your hand.

She is not happy with this picture, which is no better than her first effort – it might even be worse – but she cannot see how to make it right.

She eats her cheese sandwich, then gathers up her things and wanders along a little path above the beach. Pitted with holes and crevices, it follows the shoreline, clinging close to the edge, before petering out, leading nowhere.

She plucks and sketches a flower, and thinks about all the time – childhood evenings and weekends and holidays – spent doing next to nothing, hours spent dropping twigs in the stream just to watch them float away; hours spent lying in the grass, watching clouds drift by, trying to see faces in them, watching them morph and dissipate; hours spent sitting on kerbs waiting for something to happen. She would like to have those endless, wasted hours again.

She thinks of writing to Alex, and looks through her satchel for spare paper. She carries so much stuff with her: as well as her painting kit there is a Polaroid camera that she meant to use and hasn't yet, and two apples, forgotten and horribly bruised, and all kinds of junk. On the back of a discarded picture, with a scratchy pen, she writes *I am here!* and feels as if she were one of those teeny tiny Whos with their teeny tiny voices that only Horton can hear, crying out, 'I am here! I am here!' She fills the page, writing about the island and the house, mentioning her housemates and her attempts to paint the landscape.

She would like to write to the drama student from her life class, to tell him *I'm living the dream!* She doesn't know where he is though. She searched for him once, on the internet, but didn't find him. And anyway, she's struggling now to recall his name.

In the late afternoon, she retraces her steps along paths which return her to the dirt track. To the south, the track ascends to a tree-lined brow. There, somewhere, at the far end of the island, is the chapel that Angie mentioned. Sandra decides she will look for it tomorrow. For now, she walks north, with her satchel feeling heavy on her shoulder, the strap digging in.

At the house, dinner is being prepared and the others have started drinking. Sandra goes upstairs, where she takes out her letter to Alex and reads it through. It sounds very cheerful. She finds an envelope and a stamp and puts the letter, ready for posting, back into her satchel. The ferry will come in a few days, then her letter can be taken over to Liel and put into a post box ready to go over to the mainland. She trusts her British stamp will be valid. The slowness of communication here makes her think of Samuel Morse, many miles from home, many years ago, receiving news via a horse messenger that his wife was convalescent when in fact she was already dead. Of the speedier system he subsequently developed, the only signal Sandra knows is SOS.

She looks at her evening dress, waiting on its hanger on the back of the door. They will mock her again, but they can go hang themselves. She puts the dress on and looks at herself in the mirror. There is a smudge of paint on her face, a trace of cloud white. She rubs it off, or rubs it in, applies some lipstick, raises her chin and makes her way downstairs.

The others are already coming through from the lounge, bringing their wine glasses with them. They take their places, and Colin leads grace. When Sandra refrains from saying 'amen', a few heads turn towards her silence, and then turn away.

Colin has cooked sausages, with mashed potato and baked beans. For Sandra, there is mashed potato and baked beans: an island of mash in a sea of beans. She digs into the island with her fork. This is the kind of food on which she weaned Joe, soft food that makes Sandra think of invalids. She finds herself rather enjoying it; it is comfort food, like the suet puddings that her mother makes, and the winter stew that is Alex's speciality. The others are talking about poetry. Sandra has missed the start of the conversation, and does not try to follow the rest. But as the others finish eating, they move on to unanimously complimenting Colin on this old favourite that is so well suited to the season, and Sandra chips in to say, 'I might try making a suet pudding. My mother makes the best suet pudding in the world.'

'It's not you tomorrow though,' says Belle. 'It's Angie tomorrow.'

'I know,' says Sandra.

'You can't eat suet,' says Alan.

'You can get vegetarian suet,' says Sandra. 'There's some in the cupboard.' When she was a child, steak and kidney pudding was her absolute favourite; now, though, she might make one with Quorn and mushroom, or, failing that, leek and cheese.

Her plate is taken away and she is passed a bowl of vanilla ice cream, which makes her think of Joe's tonsillitis.

When everyone has finished and Angie is washing up, the rest of them move through to the lounge. Sandra sits down on the little sofa and pours herself a glass of wine. She notes that Angie has not packed away the game of Monopoly that she got out the night before, but that doesn't seem to stop everyone getting out more: Alan, squatting in front of the games cupboard, is merrily removing a chess board and a box of chess pieces. 'Fancy a game?' he says to Colin. Meanwhile, Belle is coming back from the cupboard with Ludo, and Harriet moves the coffee table book onto the floor to make room for it. The two of them set it up at one end of the table while the men arrange their chess board at the other. Sandra does not really want to play Ludo; it is Joe's favourite game but it can bore her to tears.

'I'll sit out,' she says.

'It's a game for four players,' says Belle.

'You can play it with three,' says Sandra. She takes her glass of wine over to the bookshelves and browses while Belle, rolling her eyes, takes a set of pieces away.

When Angie comes in, Belle says to her, 'Sandra's not playing.'

Angie does not express surprise.

The men have started moving their pawns.

'There are some good books here,' says Sandra.

'We'll roll to see who goes first,' says Belle.

Sandra prises out a book about watercolour painting. Turning the pages, studying the pictures, she says, 'I do wish I could paint like this.'

'Where's the dice?' asks Harriet.

'Here,' says Angie, passing it.

Sandra lingers the longest over the seascapes. 'I have trouble capturing depth,' she says. She looks over at the Ludo players. 'There were some very good seascapes at the gallery where Harriet and I saw a sculpture exhibition.'

'You can't go,' says Belle.

'No,' agrees Angie, frowning down at the dice, needing a six to start.

Sandra returns the book to the shelf. She can't see the Valerie Swanson biography, which someone is no doubt reading, but there is a book on the history of film, which she takes out. The first chapter deals with the silent era, beginning with Maxim Gorky's response to seeing an 1896 programme of Lumière films: *Last night, he wrote, I was in the Kingdom of Shadows. If you only knew how strange it is to be there. It is a world without sound, without colour. Everything there – the earth, the trees, the people, the water and the air – is dipped in monotonous grey. Grey rays of the sun across the grey sky, grey eyes in grey faces, and the leaves of the trees are ashen grey. It is not life but its shadow, it is not motion but its soundless spectre.* This is Valerie Swanson's world.

And here is Valerie Swanson herself, pictured, named, quoted. With a turn of the page, though, the silent era is drawing to an end – the talkies are coming. The strange, soundless and colourless world that Valerie inhabits belongs to the past. She says she is 'getting out just in time', as if it were her decision; either way, she hates the talkies, this modern world, and she is not alone: when fire destroys a Paramount studio, Clara Bow says, 'I hope to Christ it was the sound stages.'

Behind her, the game of chess ends with mate and a groan of disappointment. Sandra turns around, saying, 'I'll play the winner,' but Alan informs her they're playing the best of three.

'You're not too late to join *our* game,' says Angie.

'I think I'll just go up,' says Sandra. She takes her wine with her, looking forward to the luxury of sipping it as she reads in bed. In reality, though, with the glass of red in her hand, she finds she's scared of the white sheets. And when she settles down, the sleep she was hoping for doesn't come; she is disturbed by the noise of the others downstairs and on the stairs and on the landing, coming and going, talking and playing music into the early hours, as if they were all alone in

65

this house, as if no one were trying to sleep. Their thought-lessness infuriates her, and she says to herself in the dark, 'I *am* here,' and she tells herself that if this carries on, she will have to go downstairs and make her displeasure known.

11

LEAVING HER LUGGAGE in the middle of the hallway, Carol approaches the first of a row of closed doors. She feels as if she should knock before entering, as if she were trespassing. Behind the door, she finds a reception room, which is neat and tidy but looks a bit like a waiting room. She tries the next door along, and finds another reception room, a larger one. She moves down the hallway. There are more reception rooms than Carol would know what to do with. The house is begging for visitors, for company, but she tells it it's going to have to make do with her, at least for now. She could watch TV in one of these rooms, except there is no TV. She is pleased to see a record player, which looks painfully old but, on closer inspection, is still in working order. She will have to hunt for the records; she can only see the empty sleeves. There is a piano, though she can only play 'Chopsticks'.

She opens another door, expecting another reception room but finding a cupboard crammed with miscellany: a carpet sweeper, an ironing board, a pair of wellies in her size, a set of golf clubs; and on the shelves, dozens of boxes of golf balls, a seemingly endless supply.

She lugs her big suitcase up the stairs to another carpeted hallway and more doors, behind which are the bedrooms. All the walls - the hallways, the reception rooms, the bedrooms - have been painted magnolia, a rather nothingy colour, like a blank page onto which the buyer can stamp their own mark.

All the beds are made, and she wonders how long they have been like that, just waiting for someone to come here to sleep. She wheels her suitcase into the nearest bedroom. She has the whole house to herself; she might sleep in a different room every night.

She has, in fact, along with her jeans and jumpers, packed a sparkly frock and a pair of heels. It is not as if, alone in this house, alone on this island, she is expecting to attend any parties, but she remains hopeful that Roman will be joining her at some point. Jayne was right: she would not want to be entirely without her nice things. Jayne is always right.

She hangs her lone frock in the wardrobe and puts everything else into drawers: clothes in which she will be comfortable, clothes for all weathers.

While she is here, she might, deprived of her lunches with Jayne, lose some weight. Or she might comfort eat, and Roman said there was wine, more wine than she could possibly drink. Either way, she will end up with nothing that fits.

She returns downstairs. The kitchen is at the back of the house. She turns on the light, and runs the tap, and opens the fridge. Everything seems to be in order. She finds a kettle and boils some water to make herself a welcome cup of coffee, but has trouble locating the cups and the coffee and the teaspoons. *Treat the place as if it were your own*, said Roman, but it does not feel like her own when she does not know where anything is. She will though, when she has been here long enough.

She will no doubt find there is something that she has forgotten, something she has not thought of, but she expects that whatever she needs she might find here; there must be all sorts of things tucked away in the many rooms of this old house.

12

SANDRA WANTS TO be inspired, just like Angie was inspired by the chapel and wrote that poem that everyone said was beautiful. She wants to paint something that she can be proud of, something the others will admire, something she could bear to hang on a wall.

She goes into the kitchen, where Angie is making a pot of tea.

'Where's that chapel you mentioned?' asks Sandra, making herself some toast.

'It's at the far end of the island,' says Angie.

'But where exactly?' says Sandra.

'If you walk south,' says Angie, 'you'll see a little track leading off to the right and then another leading off to the left.'

'I've been down both those tracks,' says Sandra. 'Both those tracks lead to the sea.'

'Everything here leads to the sea,' says Angie. 'But keep going south until you reach the copse near the brow of the hill. You'll see another turn-off to your right, and at the end of that is the chapel.'

They take their breakfast things out to the garden, where Belle and Harriet are discussing the Angela Carter book, and Angie is drawn into their conversation. Sandra does her best not to listen, attending instead to her toast.

The sky is rather overcast, but when Sandra sets off, she has in mind a chapel that she saw on a sunny summer's day, on a childhood holiday somewhere: a pretty stone building, surrounded by wild flowers.

Here she is, she thinks, on her way to Valerie Swanson's private chapel, and, what's more, on a Sunday. Although here, every day feels a bit like a Sunday.

She passes the first two turn-offs, pressing on up the incline until, near the brow of the hill, she sees the third turn-off. She follows the path between the trees, and finds, in their shade, a rather unappealing building. *Is this it?* thinks Sandra. The door is grander than the building warrants. The drab walls are cold and damp and disappearing beneath a layer of algae. At the rear, a lacklustre window showcases the darkness inside. Still, she would like to go in, but she finds the door locked.

She eyes those dreary walls and thinks about the shades she must mix. Settling on a view from the front, she sits down and opens her satchel. While she works, she thinks about the chapel from that childhood holiday. She remembers pushing open the arched door and walking into the hush. She remembers the smell of the ancient stone, the ancient wood. At the far end of the aisle, there was a stained glass window depicting the Ascension, and as Sandra stood looking up at it, the clouds must have parted and the sun streamed through and in that moment it would have been possible to believe in God or in *something*, she felt such peace. And then her mother said, 'Sandra . . . *Sandra*, we have to go, your father's waiting to eat.' They ate a picnic in the meadow, and afterwards Sandra went back to the chapel, but there were too many people in there, and another girl was standing where she had stood, and it was time to go, *now, Sandra*. She remembers the walk back to the car, and the drive home.

Her angle is wrong. She has been looking at the chapel

face on, and it looks flat on the page, paper thin, like a child's drawing of a house. She will have to start again.

She eats her tomato sandwich, listening to distant birdsong, and then moves to a different spot. Still out of the sun, she is getting cold, but she makes her pencil outline and, when she is pleased with it, chooses a brush. The stone's damp grey-brown is not easy to replicate: she mixes it too grey or too brown or too dark, but eventually she is almost satisfied.

She fills the rest of the page with trees, and just glimpses of sky, and only afterwards thinks that it might have been better just to *suggest* so many trees, rather than attempting to paint in every trunk and branch. The background now overwhelms the picture; it makes her think of Macbeth's Great Birnam wood, ominous and advancing.

She regards her picture, which is not right at all. She cannot remember where it was, that sunlit chapel. Her parents would know.

Her fingers are seizing up from the cold. She ought to have worn her gloves, although then she might not have been able to paint. With her stiffening fingers, she packs away her things. She has been on the ground for so long that she aches when she stands. Painfully aware of her bones, she walks back down the path, the sun sinking behind her. She has yet to explore the southernmost end of the island, beyond the trees. For now, she heads back to the house. It is getting late, and she is half frozen, and the weak evening sun is not penetrating.

Sandra struggles, in the hallway, to bend her stone-cold fingers to undo her bootlaces, the double knot. She has to warm her hands by rubbing them and breathing on them, like Joe in his school play acting the part of someone who had been out in the snow, stamping his feet the same way he did when he did not get what he wanted. He had not wanted that part; he had wanted to be something else, though Sandra can no longer remember what.

Angie pokes her head out of the kitchen to see who has come in. She is warm from the oven, her plump cheeks pink. Emerging into the chilly hallway, she says to Sandra, 'You've brought the cold in with you.'

'Yes,' says Sandra. She could do with a warmer pair of fingers untying her laces, unbuttoning her coat.

'Did you find what you were looking for?' asks Angie.

'I found the chapel,' says Sandra. 'I'd hoped to get inside but the door was locked.'

'Yes,' says Angie. 'The key's here somewhere but I don't know where, and anyway, I'm not sure it's safe.'

'We've got the key?' says Sandra.

'I thought you were doing landscapes,' says Angie.

'I am,' says Sandra. 'I'd still like to get in.'

'Well, anyway,' says Angie, turning away, 'I'm making the dinner. It won't be long.' She returns to the warmth of the kitchen and closes the door.

Sandra is beginning to thaw now; the feeling is returning to her fingers, which are starting to hurt. Finally, the double knot is undone and her boots are off and her coat is on its peg. She can hear Alan laughing in the lounge. Sandra takes her satchel upstairs, into the bedroom, where she is annoyed to see the mess that Angie seems compelled to leave behind her everywhere she goes: the floor is decorated with saucers of ash and lipstick-stained dog-ends, and clothes and damp towels which Sandra picks up and drops onto Angie's unmade bed. She gathers up Angie's toiletries, which are strewn between the gaping mouth of her bathroom bag and the chest of drawers, where spilt cotton wool balls butt up against a wine

72

glass with a finger of red in the bottom. She steps on the hard plastic spikes of a hairbrush and swears at it as she kicks it into a corner, knocking the wine glass over. The dregs slosh out, red wine dashing the pale floorboards and leaking through the gaps between them.

She can hear Angie calling everyone through to dinner, and *that bloody saucepan*, she thinks, *that bloody spoon*. It's a horrible noise and Sandra wants it to stop. 'All right, all right,' she says, though no one can hear her. 'I'm coming.' She changes into her dress and goes downstairs. Everyone is filing into the kitchen, wine glasses in hand. 'Steak and kidney pudding tonight,' announces Angie.

Sandra looks at the dish on the table. 'I was going to make a suet pudding tomorrow,' she says.

'We won't want it tonight *and* tomorrow,' says Belle.

'But I *said* I was going to make it tomorrow,' says Sandra.

'You said you *might*,' says Alan.

'But Angie's made one,' says Harriet. 'You can make something else.'

The others sit down. Sandra goes to the wine rack and removes a bottle of wine. While Angie leads grace, Sandra pours herself a glass, and when the others say, 'Amen,' Sandra takes a gulp of this middling homemade wine.

Angie serves out the steak and kidney pudding, and passes Sandra a cheese salad from the fridge. 'Help yourself to cabbage,' she says.

When everyone else has gone through to the lounge, Sandra scrapes the scraps of steak and kidney pudding off the plates, into the bin. Not that there is much to scrape: Angie's suet pudding went down well. While the sink fills with hot, soapy water, Sandra finishes her wine. She tells herself that they would have liked her own suet pudding just as much. She will tell her mother about this, about Angie knowing that Sandra wanted to make a suet pudding and then making one herself; she looks forward to telling her, and to her mother taking her side, and feeling vindicated. At least, she hopes her mother would take her side. She might not. She might just tell her to grow up.

The state in which Angie has left the work surfaces is unbelievable. 'Did you have to make *such* a mess,' she mutters, looking at the thick dust of flour, the sticky blobs of dough. It is going to be a nightmare to clear up.

When she is finally satisfied, or as close as she is likely to get, Sandra takes her wine glass through to the lounge and fills it from the bottle that is open on the coffee table, on top of the Monopoly board. Crowded around it are various bulging brown paper bags that make her think of panic attacks. She leans forward and peers into one: it is full of custard tarts. Another contains brown sugar sponge.

'She wants something now,' says Alan.

'What would you like, Sandra?' asks Harriet.

'Where did they come from?' asks Sandra.

'They came on the Sunday ferry,' says Angie. 'They were delivered this afternoon.'

'I thought there was only the Wednesday ferry,' says Sandra.

'Wednesday and Sunday,' says Angie.

'I wanted to see him,' says Sandra, thinking of the letter still stashed in her satchel when it could have been on its way by now.

'Well,' says Belle, 'you missed him.' She has a knife in her hand and is cutting into the brown sugar sponge. 'Who wants some?' she asks.

Everyone wants some, although Sandra, who has no

goodies of her own to offer in return, says, 'Just a small piece.' Belle cuts five good pieces and a sliver for Sandra.

'Who'd like some buttermilk pie?' asks Angie. She slices it up, with just a taste for Sandra.

'I might order something for next time,' says Sandra.

'He's already taken the orders for Wednesday,' says Belle.

The six plates are handed out, along with forks. The table's a mess of bottles and glasses and bags and sticky knives and crumbs and spilt sugar, not to mention Alan's inside-out socks. If they're not careful, they'll have ants to deal with.

'Angie,' says Sandra, 'I found a dirty wine glass in the bedroom. It's probably not a good idea to leave things like that up there, where they can get knocked over. We don't want to be paying for breakages and damage.'

'I agree,' says Angie, 'but I haven't taken a wine glass up to the bedroom.'

'Well, it was there,' says Sandra.

Belle says to Sandra, 'Perhaps it was yours.'

Sandra, realising in that moment that the wine glass was indeed the one she had taken upstairs the previous night and left unfinished on the floor, lets the matter drop. She glances at the ceiling, as if she might see the red wine seeping through from above, the ceiling stained, but there is nothing to see.

She turns her attention to the chess board and the higgledy-piggledy pieces which she sets about sorting onto their squares, and when she has finished she discovers no one wants to play. 'Well then,' she says, annoyed, 'perhaps it could be put away.' She looks at Alan, who got it out in the first place, but he shows no sign of having heard her. She looks at Colin, who gets up and goes to the record player. He puts on 'Then I'll Be Happy' and Sandra says, 'Do we have to have this again?' but is shushed. They sit quietly and listen, while Sandra scrapes up her mean pieces of cake, the tines of her fork scratching her plate like fingernails on a blackboard.

13

ONCE A WEEK, the ferryman leaves Carol's groceries in a waterproof storage container at her end of the jetty. He won't come up to the house. If Carol sees the ferry coming over from Liel, she goes out to the jetty to meet him; she invites him in for coffee but he always refuses. He does not seem displeased to see her, and asks if she is all right, but he won't come in, and does not linger. Sometimes, she finds that he has come and gone without her noticing, and what was an empty plastic tub is now miraculously packed with supplies, like a Christmas stocking filled by an unseen Santa.

Along with the groceries, the ferryman brings Carol's mail: her subscription magazines, and books she has ordered even though it would take an eternity to read everything she wants to read. Even here, the junk mail finds her. And there are letters from Jayne, who asks if Carol's enjoying her 'self-imposed exile', and who sends news and anecdotes to tempt Carol home with everything she is missing. At the bottom of an advert for a new jazz bar in the city, Jayne has written, *How's the night life there?* She encloses comparative weather reports showing rain where Carol is and sunshine at home, and stories set on islands, novels – by Agatha Christie and H.G. Wells and William Golding – in which things take a nasty turn.

Carol has something close to a routine now. In the mornings, she is up by eight o'clock, and has a good breakfast with plenty of coffee. Afterwards, she walks around the island, which does not take long but it blows away the cobwebs. Then she writes. She writes on her laptop in one of the reception rooms. And she does finally feel that she is getting somewhere. It is not just the seclusion, the lack of distraction; the very strangeness of this place seems to have unlocked something in her. Slowly but surely, a story is taking shape. She writes without looking back at what she's done; she will not go back to the start until she reaches the end.

She breaks when she is hungry. She has established certain boundaries which she thinks will help her here, such as not writing while she is eating, and not forgetting to go outside from time to time. When she is done for the day, she might go out and hit some golf balls into the sea, though she is already running out; she will have to be careful.

Each evening, she fixes herself a quick supper in the over-size, echoey kitchen. There is, as promised, plenty of wine, but it is rather rough. She reads, and writes letters for the ferryman to take. There is a phone in the house but it doesn't seem to be working. She has no internet. She plays 'Chopsticks' on the piano, which sounds so loud in this house that is other-wise quiet, apart from the wind moaning down the chimneys, and the ceaseless sound of the sea which presses in on every side.

She struggles most when it starts to get dark, when another day is over, or another week, and still she might have months left to go, and thinking this, she feels like a prisoner in a film, as if she ought to be tallying the days on the wall of her cell. When it is time to go up to bed, she turns off the lights in the reception room, and in the kitchen, and at the top of the stairs. The sea, through every window, looks black.

14

SANDRA IS UP first, leaving Angie snoring. There is no one in the bathroom, no one in the kitchen, no one in the lounge. By the time she hears anyone moving upstairs – a bedroom door opening, the bathroom light pinging on – she is in the hallway, putting on her trainers.

She is desperate to run. She has not been out for a run since Thursday, and now it is Monday. She looks for her gloves, the bright pink gloves that keep her safe on the roads, finds them in the pouch of her sweatshirt and pulls them on.

Outside, with her Walkman on, she jogs towards the dock. Entering the woodland, she thinks of the birds they heard singing when they arrived, the shrike Colin hoped he was listening to, but if it is there she can't see it, and she wouldn't be able to hear it through this power ballad.

The dirt track emerges from the woods and stops at the jetty. From the house to here is about the same distance as she has to walk – or run – from her front door to Joe's primary school. She feels as if she's in training for home time, for which she is so often late.

It is a surprisingly mild morning and her hands are hot. She takes off her gloves before heading back into the woods. She is planning on doing a mile or two before breakfast, and then, she thinks, she will be set for the day, but when she reaches the house she sees Belle in the doorway, watching for her, calling her in. 'I'm running,' says Sandra, coming to a stop, removing her headphones.

'That's good,' says Belle. 'It will improve your creativity, and your mood.'

'But you stopped me,' says Sandra.

'Have you seen the Josephine Baker record?' asks Belle. 'Colin's looking for it. He says he left it on the turntable last night and now it's gone.'

Angie calls down from the landing, 'Are you in or out, Sandra? All the cold's coming in.'

Belle brings Sandra into the hallway and closes the door behind her. 'The sleeve's still there,' she says, 'but it's empty.'

Colin pokes his head out of the lounge to ask if Sandra knows anything about it, and Sandra is maneuvered towards the lounge to witness the search. 'Take your shoes off then,' says Belle.

'Here it is,' says Harriet, fetching the record down from its hiding place on the highest shelf.

'How did it get up there?' asks Alan.

'Is it all right?' asks Colin, taking it carefully from Harriet, checking it for scratches. He returns it to the turntable and sets it playing, before Sandra's even had breakfast. She leaves them to it, pulling the lounge door to and going through to the kitchen.

She makes herself a mug of tea. There is a plate of croissants on the table and Sandra takes one, eating it over the sink, without butter, without jam or cheese. She drinks her tea, looking out of the window at the quality of the light. There is no sunshine to speak of but they have not had a really bad day yet.

She goes upstairs and showers, thinking about how she might spend her day. She sees no point in going back to the chapel if she cannot get inside: she has already done the exterior, and she has done the view to the east and west of the island. She does not want to try again, to do the same thing, badly, over and over.

Her painting clothes are starting to feel dirty but she puts them on, picks up her satchel and heads out. She did tell herself that at some point she would paint the view to the north, Liel in the distance. She sets off for the dock. As she enters the woods, she thinks about all the creatures that must live here unseen, in holes in the trees and holes in the ground, under logs and rocks and fallen leaves. Back home, there is a museum that Joe has always liked, and in particular he likes those little doors that can be opened to reveal a bird or a mammal or an insect, all dead of course. Sandra is not so keen.

She sees movement in the distance, which turns out to be Colin, deep in the woodland, in his camouflage. He seems to see her but does not return her wave – he is holding something in his cupped hands. It will be one of his found objects, some little thing he wants to keep.

Reaching the dock, Sandra finds she cannot, in fact, see Liel through the fog that has gathered in between the two islands. Nevertheless, she sits down at the end of the jetty and readies herself to tackle this seascape, this fogscape, opening her paint set, filling her water pot, turning to a clean page in her watercolour pad. She hardly needs her pencil, just different concentrations of grey. She wets the page and paints the sunless sky, and the miles of bare sea. Even as she is doing it, she knows it is no good; there is no focal point. She decides to wait for Liel to become visible, and in the meantime she takes her lunch out of her bag.

Hearing someone approaching behind her, she turns and sees Harriet coming down the dirt track in her lurid mac.

Harriet comes right up to where Sandra is sitting and, standing above her, asks, 'Are you happy with what you've done?'

'What?' says Sandra.

Harriet gestures towards Sandra's painting and says, 'Are you happy with it?'

'Not really,' says Sandra. 'I don't seem to be getting any better.'

'Well,' says Harriet, 'it takes ten thousand hours, doesn't it?'

Sandra has heard this, and wonders if it is true. If, when she gets back to the mainland, she could devote a couple of hours each Sunday to painting, it would take her – she tries to do the sum in her head – close to a hundred years. Or every Saturday and Sunday morning, every weekend: that would be more like thirty years. And even then, what if it just did not happen; what if, after ten thousand hours, what she'd been working towards still eluded her? She would be an old lady with thousands of disappointing seas.

'Landscapes don't interest me,' says Harriet. 'I'm more interested in people.'

Sandra puts the last bit of crust into her mouth and shrugs.

'I'll see you later,' says Harriet, wandering away in the direction of the woods.

Sandra looks back towards Liel. She must be right opposite the Sea View hotel. She imagines herself peering from the dining room window or from the docks, trying to see what is over here. Even with binoculars, she would be unable to see through this veil of fog, which shows no sign of lifting.

The light is going. She has no idea what time it is, but it must be getting late. Were it not for the fog, she might have been able to see lights on Liel, twinkling like stars.

The tide will be coming in; the rising water will flood

the jetty, right where she is sitting, so she had better move. Besides, it is her turn to cook.

Sandra packs everything away in her satchel and walks back down the dirt track to the house. She has not decided what she is going to make for dinner. She cannot make the suet pudding now. Perhaps a stew, she thinks, or a pie. Something warming and comforting for the autumn.

When she opens the front door, she finds the others standing in the hallway, taking off their outdoor things. 'We were expecting you to be here already,' says Belle. 'It's your turn to cook. Had you forgotten?'

'No,' says Sandra. 'I hadn't forgotten.'

'She *had* forgotten,' says Alan.

'I *hadn't* forgotten,' says Sandra, bending down to begin unlacing her boots while the others take a bottle of wine and five glasses into the lounge, closing the door behind them to keep out the chill. Leaving her satchel downstairs, hung up with her coat, Sandra goes into the kitchen. It is cold in there too but it will soon warm up with the oven on.

Rummaging through the cupboards, she decides on lasagne, and takes out a box of pasta, tinned tomatoes, an onion. The fridge has been magically replenished since she last looked: as well as cheese, mushrooms, peppers, courgettes, there are new eggs.

She opens a bottle of wine for herself and pours a generous measure, wishing she had a radio for company.

Belle takes her seat at the head of the table and says, 'What's this then?'

'Lasagne,' says Sandra.

'Oh, I like lasagne,' says Angie.

Sandra shovels limp slabs of it onto the plates she has

warmed and hands them around the table. 'There's plenty more,' she says, 'if anyone wants it.' She picks up her cutlery.

'Aren't you going to say grace?' prompts Belle.

Sandra nods. She can say it, even if she does not believe in it, in a god who feeds her, who hears her when she speaks. She can say the grace of her childhood, of the school dining hall, spoken by the server – *For what we are about to receive, may the Lord make us truly thankful* – before spooning out the bony fish, the dyed-green peas. Sandra was never a server. She didn't know how a girl became one: they just seemed to be chosen, privately, secretly. Sandra was never chosen.

'For what we are about to receive,' says Sandra, 'may the Lord make us truly thankful,' and the others say, 'Amen.'

She has begun to eat when Alan says, 'Where's the meat?'

Sandra swallows her mouthful and says, 'It's vegetarian.'

'But lasagne's supposed to have meat in it,' says Angie. 'Mince.'

'This one's vegetarian,' says Sandra.

'But we all eat meat,' says Alan.

'I know,' says Sandra, 'but you can eat something without meat in it, can't you?'

'*You're* vegetarian,' says Alan, 'so we've been giving *you*, every evening, a special vegetarian meal. We haven't forced you to eat meat. But we're not vegetarian, so it would have been fair, don't you think, for us to get meat, not to be forced to eat vegetarian food.'

Sandra looks around the table at the others, and sees that they all agree with him. 'Well, it's done now,' she says. She continues eating, and after a while the others grudgingly pick up their cutlery and make the best of it, with the exception of Alan, who pushes away his plate and fetches himself a bag of cheese and onion crisps. He opens them with unnecessary ostentation and eats the first crisp with great relish before making a big performance of offering them around the table. Sandra, despite disliking their smell, makes a point of accepting one, just as he ought to eat her lasagne. 'You're happy enough eating these crisps,' she points out, licking her fingers, 'and *they*'re vegetarian.'

'They're not actually,' says Alan. 'They're made with animal rennet.'

Sandra refuses to give him satisfaction. She looks away, and sips her water, feeling the wet crisps jammed in the nooks and crannies of her teeth.

At the other end of the table, Belle is discussing her work with Angie and Harriet, both of whom already seem to be familiar with it. Sandra does not have a clue what Belle does, but it appears she has been recording the sound of the wind onto cassette tapes. She imagines Belle's exhibitions, rooms containing no paintings, just the faint *sound* of painting.

'It's not easy, though, is it?' says Harriet. 'Look at Sandra. She spends hours on those paintings.' She turns and looks down the table at Sandra. 'Don't you? And you're not happy with any of it, with anything you've done.'

Angie says she would like to see what Sandra's been doing, and so, after their ice cream, as they pass through the hallway, Sandra fetches her watercolour pad from her satchel. Angie sits down, with a drink in her hand, and looks steadily through Sandra's work, murmuring sympathetically. 'Yes,' she says finally, handing it back, 'I see what you mean.'

At least Colin seems to have got the message and for once has not put on that record. Instead, he is sitting quietly with a book of photographs of Natural History Museum exhibits. When Angie gets up and crosses the room, Sandra watches her, thinking she is going to the games cupboard. If Angie comes back with Twister, Sandra will leave. But Angie goes to the bookshelves and comes back with some poetry, Sylvia Plath. Alan wanders over too, making an approving comment about the excellent library. He spends a few minutes browsing and then sits down with a book on Bauhaus architecture, getting his reading glasses out of his breast pocket, while Harriet fetches down one of the Mapplethorpes. Sandra gets up and picks out a book on watercolour flowers and takes it back to her seat. When Belle comes in from the kitchen, she looks around the room and pauses only to top up each of the wine glasses before going to the shelves for a book to bring back to her armchair, settling into the companionable silence.

Sandra, relaxing, thinks how pleasant this is, to sit quietly together, the only sounds the occasional turning of a page, and the swallowing of wine, and the rhythm of breathing, which reminds her of the yoga she is missing. She could fall asleep like this. She wants to put her feet up on the sofa but stays still. 'If this isn't nice,' she says, 'I don't know what is.'

'Shh,' says Belle.

'Let's have some background music,' says Colin, getting to his feet.

15

EVERY MORNING, CAROL lights a fire in the reception room in which she writes. Even so, it can be arctic inside this big old house, and she is often forced to work with gloves on. There is no central heating here, no electric heater, nothing like that. There is not much in the way of appliances. There is no washing machine. She washes her clothes and bedding by hand in the claw-footed bath. It is hard work: she feels like a woman from another century, bent over a washboard, her back going, her hands coarsening. She dries her laundry in the sunshine or the wind, on a line strung between two apple trees.

Her standards are slipping. If her clothes are not quite clean, she wears them anyway; she can always wash them tomorrow. She is out of shampoo and is waiting for more, and if, in the meantime, her hair is a mess, she doesn't really care. If she doesn't feel like washing up at the end of the day – and, to be honest, after dark, the kitchen creeps her out – she just leaves it.

She has been trying out the other bedrooms, but most of them have those same magnolia walls, the same neutral carpets and curtains and bedding, so she is going to all the trouble of moving into a new room and finding it's really no different except maybe smaller or with less cupboard space. At least the bedding is clean. There is one room which is very pretty, with the bed right beneath a picture window, but which is just unbearable to be in; it is desperately chilly, the sheets as cold as stone, and even under an extra blanket, even wearing a jumper all night, Carol cannot get warm in there.

At the far end of the upstairs hallway is the master bedroom, distinguished from the others by a colour scheme fit for a queen, though it is all rather shabby, untouched by the decorators. There is a chandelier hanging from the high ceiling, and a four-poster bed, whose mattress is invitingly soft. Carol can almost imagine the personality of this room's owner, though all personal effects have been removed: there is nothing on the vanity table, nothing in the drawers, no photograph of a loved one on the bedside table, no pictures on the walls, just holes where they once hung. There is a bay window overlooking the sea. Of course, there is not a room in the house that does not have a view of the sea. It is the most beautiful room but Carol cannot sleep in it because of the strange, garlicky smell. It makes her feel quite faint, like an old-fashioned lady in need of smelling salts. She has tried raising the sash window to air the room, but the window, no doubt loose in a rotting frame, slams back down, and she has found no way to keep it open.

She returns to what she thinks of as her own room, the first room she slept in, right at the top of the stairs and furthest from the master bedroom. At the same time, she has started coming to bed later, keeping the lights blazing and playing 'Chopsticks' over and over, as if the light and the noise might be keeping something at bay. And even when she goes to sleep, she leaves a light on, as if she were a child, scared of the dark. Although, as she used to insist when she was little, she wasn't scared of the dark; she was only scared of what was *in* the dark.

16

SANDRA DREAMS SHE is at home, about to go for a run. When she wakes in the white room, she's confused, until she hears snoring. Sitting up, she bangs her head on the ceiling. Angie sleeps through the swearing until Sandra, getting out of bed, puts her weight on that same spiky hairbrush.

Sandra gets into the shower before Angie can. When she returns to the bedroom, she finds Angie talking to Alan, who is standing inches from Sandra's pillow eating cheese and onion crisps. Even after he leaves, the smell remains. Sandra opens the window, but Angie says she wants it closed, and closes it. 'It's on *my* side of the room,' says Angie. As soon as Angie goes to the bathroom, Sandra opens the window again and then dresses in her painting clothes, which she could have washed last night.

Sandra is on the stairs when she hears the bathroom door opening, followed by the sound of the bedroom window slamming shut.

In the kitchen, she finds the leftover croissants out on the table with the rest of the breakfast things, and she takes one.

'You're having a croissant, are you?' says Alan.

'Yes,' says Sandra, tearing it open. 'I'm sure they're still fine.' She reaches for a knife and spreads on some jam.

'They are,' says Alan. 'But I hadn't realised you'd ordered one.'

'Ordered one?' says Sandra.

'You have to order them,' says Alan. 'Did you have one yesterday as well?'

'Yes,' says Sandra.

'I suspected it was you,' says Alan. 'But the others defended you.'

Belle comes into the kitchen and puts the kettle on. Alan tells her, 'I've found our culprit.' He is pointing at Sandra, who still has the jammy knife in her hand.

'Sandra,' says Belle, 'you're very welcome to a croissant. You just had to ask.'

'It's common courtesy,' says Alan. He carries his coffee out of the kitchen, while Sandra bites into her croissant.

Belle puts a fistful of teabags into the teapot and says to Sandra, 'If you didn't order a pastry, there's toast or cereal.'

'I didn't know we had to order them,' says Sandra.

Belle empties the kettle into the teapot and takes two clean mugs from the mug tree. Sandra follows her outside. Sitting down at the picnic table with her sticky croissant, her sticky mouth, she is aware of looks being exchanged.

'She thought it was all right to take it,' says Belle, setting down the mugs and filling them from the fresh pot of tea. She hands one to Sandra and passes the milk.

'You have to order them,' says Harriet.

'I know,' says Sandra. 'I'll order some on Wednesday, when the ferry comes.'

When breakfast is over, they all bring their dishes into the kitchen and then bustle about in the hallway putting on their outdoor things. It is only then that Sandra notices her watercolour pad lying on the floor near the boots, a dirty bootprint stamped neatly across yesterday's work. She bends down to pick up her spoiled picture. 'Look at this,' she says, showing it around. It looks deliberate, like a statement about art, or about her art at least.

'Oh dear,' says Angie.

'It's not a good idea to leave your stuff lying around,' says Harriet.

'Better to look after your things,' agrees Angie.

'I put it back in my satchel,' says Sandra. 'I'm sure I did.'

'You can't have done,' says Harriet, gesturing to the evidence.

'You weren't very happy with it anyway,' says Colin, 'were you?'

While the others head out, Sandra stays behind to try and salvage her picture, to clean off the layer of dirt without damaging what's underneath. She thinks of conservators who work painstakingly to reveal a painting's original glory, and who sometimes discover paintings beneath paintings, removing work deemed dispensable so as to get at something more valuable. She wonders if they ever regret it, if they find they like the painting underneath somewhat less. The bootprint will not come off anyway, and so she must leave it, with her miserable view of Liel peeking through.

When she eventually gets outside, she pauses, not knowing which way she should turn. Directly opposite the house, half hidden by the hedge, is a stile. She climbs over, pushing through the overgrowth, and finds, on the far side, a rather lovely meadow, beyond which must be sea. She looks for a bull or bullocks or cows, none of which she would wish to encounter, none of which she can see though; of course, there would be no one here to care for them.

She wades through the tall grass and wild flowers, looking for an exit, finding another obscured stile that brings her to the most beautiful bay. There is a stretch of fine, clean sand to her left, and, to her right, what must be that same tumble of boulders she saw from the other side; it is as if, just the other day, she was standing outside a secret room and has now unwittingly found her way in.

She takes off her boots and socks and, with the sand massaging the soles of her feet, pushing in between her toes, walks a little way along the beach, looking for the perfect place in which to sit, though it is all much of a muchness. She chooses a spot, opens her satchel and unpacks her things, including the Polaroid camera. She assumes she will want photographs, to remember this place. Also, she might want to work on her paintings later, when she is no longer here.

She aims the viewfinder at the shore and presses the button. She has always loved Polaroids. Within moments, she sees the picture forming on the photographic paper, the colours filling in. It's a good picture, nice and straight, with sand and sea and sky in neat thirds, layered like rock strata.

She fastens it to the corner of her page and sets to work.

She has had to discard a few false starts, but, she thinks, squinting at her painting in the failing light, she has something here that she could nearly be satisfied with. This attempt might be far from perfect but she cannot really see how to improve it. It does need something – a detail, a touch of light, or shade. The tip of her brush hovers over her palette. But it is getting late and she ought to be getting back to the house for dinner. She rinses and dries her brush and pours her dirty water into the cold sand.

Entering the house, Sandra is greeted by Belle calling out, 'You're late! We started without you.' Sandra shuts the door behind her, smelling Stilton and garlic.

❧

92

An hour later, in the lounge, the smell of garlic is still strong. Sandra opens a window but Angie wants it closed again, and Belle says, 'Close it, Sandra, Angie's in a delicate condition.' Sandra shuts it with a bang. Belle says to her, 'You've still not told us where you were all day,' as though anyone's asked.

'It must have been something good to make you late for dinner,' says Alan.

'I found a very nice bay,' says Sandra. She fetches her watercolour pad and shows Belle the painting she did.

'Oh, that's beautiful,' says Belle.

The Polaroid is still attached to the corner of the page, and Sandra says, 'When I had my exhibition, I found myself looking at the work I'd got on display and feeling that I'd not got it quite right but not really knowing what was wrong. So at the bay today I took a photo for comparison.'

'Oh yes,' says Angie, leaning in to look. 'Beautiful.'

'Thank you,' says Sandra. 'I wasn't sure I'd quite done it justice.'

'Well,' says Belle, looking at her pallid sand, her thin sea, 'no. But it looks lovely in the photo.'

'We should go there tomorrow,' says Harriet. 'We'll go swimming in the sea, and have our lunch on the beach.'

'Good idea,' says Belle, reaching for the wine bottle, filling up their glasses.

The table's still a mess. 'The Monopoly's still out,' says Sandra.

'Yes!' says Angie, sitting forward. 'Do you want to play?'

'No,' says Sandra.

Angie sighs and turns her attention to something she's been knitting for the baby, which is due in November, and Belle says she's cutting it fine. 'I'm on the sleeves,' says Angie, holding up the tiny sky-blue cardigan.

'I mean being here,' says Belle. 'The baby might come early.'

'But we'd be here to help,' says Colin. 'We'd look after it.' He looks over at the record player and starts to get up. *If he plays that bloody song one more time*, thinks Sandra. It's too late anyway: a year from now – *decades* from now – she will still have it stuck in her head.

17

CAROL IS WAKING later and later, and still feels half asleep when she goes down to the kitchen to put the kettle on. Normally, she is confronted by yesterday's mess and the need to deal with it, but this morning she finds that her washing up has been done, the table and the counters have been wiped clean. She thinks back to the previous evening, but is quite sure that when she went to bed she left it all undone. It is, frankly, frightening, as if she has been visited by the elves from 'The Elves and the Shoemaker', a story that always struck her as rather sinister. She would not want those elves in her house, sneaking about with big scissors while she was sleeping, leaving behind all those shoes that they insisted on making in the small hours.

There is a vase of flowers on the dresser. The crackle glaze vase was there before, but not the flowers, which are fresh, as if they have bloomed from nothing overnight. Drawing nearer, she discovers a handwritten note left by Roman, who has come to see her. He says he hopes she is well, and that he is waiting outside.

He is sitting on the bench at the front of the house, wrapped up warm. He greets her with delight. 'You are looking well!' he says, and she wonders if he means that she has put on weight, which she has.

'What are you doing out here?' she says. 'Come in, have some coffee.'

'No, no,' he says. 'I prefer to be out here. I've brought breakfast with me; I've even brought coffee.' He shows her his little hamper, complete with a flask and crockery and cutlery and napkins and everything they could possibly need. He asks if the wasps have been troubling her. 'They can be a nuisance.'

'I haven't noticed any,' says Carol.

'Well,' says Roman, 'perhaps they've decided to leave you alone.' He gets out the food. 'I would have told you I was coming but the phone isn't working.'

'No,' says Carol. 'It wasn't working when I arrived.'

'I'll get someone to look at that,' says Roman.

They sit together on the bench and have their breakfast, watching out for wasps and gulls. Roman asks how the novel is coming along and Carol tells him she's making good progress. She tells him the basic idea and he looks bemused.

They take a walk, circling the house. 'Whoever buys this place will have their work cut out for them,' says Roman, looking up at the broken guttering, the slipping tiles. Despite the spruced-up paintwork, the superficial primping, the house has underlying problems.

When they come to the back of the house, he frowns down at the weeds that are choking the vegetable patch, and Carol wonders if she was supposed to take care of that sort of thing, if maintaining the house was an unspoken part of the deal. The blackberry bushes are growing thick against the west-facing wall, and Carol thinks of Sleeping Beauty, asleep for years, a hundred years, behind the brambles. That fairy tale's out of favour now, because of a kiss the princess may not have wanted but was unable to resist.

'Someone is interested though,' says Roman.

'Someone's interested in buying?' says Carol. A small part of her might be relieved to be told she was to pack her bags immediately, to board Roman's boat, to be taken home, with her work still unfinished, but her overriding desire is to stay. When it comes to it, she won't find it easy to leave.

'Whatever happens is not going to happen yet,' says Roman.

Carol accepts this. 'Let's go inside,' she says. 'I'll light a fire. I'll show you what I've written. I'll make us some lunch.' She wonders if he is going to stay overnight. If he sleeps here, he will find out she snores.

But Roman says he won't stay. Like the ferryman, he is keen to get going. 'Things to do, people to see,' he says. 'On the mainland.'

'Of course,' says Carol.

'And you'll want to get back to your novel,' he adds.

'Absolutely,' says Carol, though she doubts she'll get started any time soon. Roman's visit has interfered with her routine. It is a minor disruption, in the scheme of things, but it is nonetheless distracting. She is, it seems, getting set in her ways on this little island, in this little bubble.

'And time,' says Roman, collecting his hamper, 'is ticking.'

Carol walks with him down to the jetty, where his motorboat is waiting. After waving him off, she walks back to the house, where she hunts around for gardening gloves. She spends the morning weeding the vegetable patch and turning the soil, leaving it bare and expectant. She might ask the ferryman to bring her some seedlings, and considers tomatoes, which are easy but susceptible to pests. Thinking, though, that she will not be here long enough to watch anything grow, she goes inside to prepare an early lunch.

18

THE OTHERS ARE up making plans. They will walk to the bay with whatever materials or equipment they need to practise their art, and they will have a picnic lunch, and they will go swimming. They will spend the whole day there and come back to the house when it is time for the evening meal.

'But I haven't brought my swimming costume,' says Angie.

'Nor have I,' says Belle. 'We'll have to go skinny dipping.'

'Oh! All right!' says Angie.

'Are you running again, Sandra?' asks Harriet, seeing Sandra in the hallway in her sweatshirt and leggings.

'Yes,' says Sandra.

'We're going down to the bay after breakfast,' says Angie.

'Yes,' says Sandra. 'I can always join you later.'

'We're going skinny dipping!' says Angie.

'Does that include the men?' asks Colin.

'All of us,' says Belle. 'You wanted a colony, didn't you, Sandra? We shall be a nudist colony! Anyone refusing to go skinny dipping will not be admitted to the bay.'

'It's a bit cold for skinny dipping,' says Sandra.

'You're not a prude, are you?' says Harriet.

'No,' says Sandra, searching her coat pockets, looking around the hallway. 'I'm just cold. Has anyone seen my gloves?' She cannot find them anywhere. They are not in the pouch of her sweatshirt. She has already looked in her room and in her satchel. No one, it seems, has seen them, and in the end she has to run without them.

Even if her fingers are cold, it feels good to run. The verge to her right, in the shade of the hedge, is silvery with frost; to her left, the sunlit grass is lushly green. She feels as if she were in between two worlds, as if she could step from winter to summer, or from summer to winter, if she chose.

Before the track runs out at the far edge of the woods, she turns and runs back towards the house. She remembers thinking, when she arrived, that this looked like home. She cannot see it now; it looks nothing like home.

Nearing the house, she sees the front door standing open, and the five of them all jammed into the hallway. She can hear their jolly voices. She runs on along the dirt track, which stretches like a spine down the middle of the island. The jetty would be the tail, she decides; the island is facing away from Liel and home, and she is running towards the head, the mouth end.

She runs up the incline, and when she reaches the copse and the little track that leads to the chapel, she comes to a stop. *The key's here somewhere.* She turns around: from here, she can see the house, and the last of the group going over the stile into the meadow. She does not want to join them, to go skinny dipping, to be naked among them. And it *will* be far too cold. Besides, the ferry is coming today; she wants to meet it, to send her letter.

She walks back to the empty house. After taking off her running shoes, she goes into the kitchen and helps herself to a croissant, which is a little stale, and then goes upstairs to take a shower. When she comes back down, fat brown paper bags have appeared on the kitchen table. 'Goddamnit,' she says, opening them up to look at the fresh bakery items. The ferry must have come early; the man must have been and gone while she was showering. Hurrying to put on her boots and her coat, grabbing her satchel, Sandra runs down to the dock, emerging from the woods to see the ferry in the distance, already miles away.

She is not happy that her letter home is still here, still on the island, when it ought to have left already. At this rate, by the time Alex receives it, the retreat will be over; he will read her letter saying *I am here!* when she no longer is. She cannot understand the ferry coming so early: it is the same ferry, the Wednesday ferry, the noon ferry, that brought them over last week.

She has been here a whole week then, though she feels as if she has been away from home for ever. She has achieved very little really; she has barely begun. At the same time, she has had quite enough. They have been lucky with the weather though. It is no doubt nicest in the summer but they have not had to spend any time confined to the house by rain and it has never been so cold that she could not get a day's work done. She ought to count her blessings.

She returns to the house. Starting in the lounge, she searches through the drawers, and while she is there she relieves the turntable of the Josephine Baker record. She has had quite enough of that too. There are limits. She hopes she never hears it again.

From there, she goes through to the kitchen, where, in a big drawer of junk, she finds what she has been looking for: a set of keys, a pair, long and rusty, one with a paper label attached, *chapel* written in a spidery hand. She slips the keys into her coat pocket, then packs up some lunch and goes out, heading south along the dirt track. She is getting a bit sick of trudging these same few hundred yards, but if she can just get into the chapel, she will be satisfied. She will not touch anything, and she will not stay long.

At the third turn-off, she heads into the trees and follows the path to the imposing door of the dingy chapel. She takes the key from her pocket. The lock is just as rusty, but the door opens, letting her into the gloomy interior of this neglected little building. There is no electric light, and what little daylight gets through the trees struggles to get through the doorway. The ceiling is high but full of shadows. The window might be better with the sun behind it, light flooding in through the coloured glass panels. But even if the sun were on the correct side of the building, the trees would always be in the way. She stands in the heavy silence, as if waiting for something.

The chapel is, all in all, a great disappointment. She makes her way out, slamming shut the heavy door, and something inside the chapel creaks ominously. She turns the key in the lock and walks back down the path.

Now what? she thinks. Back at the dirt track, she pauses. She has seen almost everything there is to see on this small island, except for the south shore. She turns right, thinking that at least all this is nearly over; she just has to get through the remaining days until it is time to go home.

She reaches the top of the incline and the far side of the copse. A stretch of grass, a gentle slope, ends suddenly; a little sign warns her to stay away from the edge, which could crumble at any time. Sandra was expecting to see, beyond this island, only sea stretching into the distance, but there is another island, a smaller one, not far away. On the facing shore, there's a jetty, and a rather incongruous pair of palm trees, arching together to form a gateway of sorts; they make the island look tropical, like some kind of exotic paradise. The little island is dominated by a grand white house which might be showing its age but which is still striking. She used to want to live in the houses she saw pictured on chocolate box lids, cottages that were inseparable from that sweet smell, like gingerbread houses. This house looks nothing like those long-ago fairy-tale cottages, but it has the same kind of appeal. She would like to try to capture it on the page.

She sits down in the grass and unpacks her lunch. She has not even taken a bite before a gull swoops in from behind and snatches the macaroni cheese pie right out of her hand, and, while she is busy yelling at it, another one comes for her treacle scone. 'All right,' she tells them, though they have already gone, 'you win.' She gets to her feet. Today, she will forage for fruit; it will be her lunch and her work for the day, some still life. Tomorrow, she will come back to paint this view; after all, she thinks, gazing admiringly at the little island, it deserves a whole day.

At the end of the afternoon, with too many imperfect apples in her stomach and on the pages of her scrapbook, Sandra returns to the house. As she comes in through the front door, Harriet comes out of the kitchen and says to Sandra, 'We ate early tonight. We were hungry.'

Belle is coming down the stairs and says to Harriet, 'Is Sandra washing up?'

'We decided to let her off,' says Harriet.

Sandra, who is squatting to take off her boots, looks up. 'It's not my night to wash up anyway,' she says.

Harriet turns and looks at Sandra. 'No,' she says, 'not you. The new Sandra.'

'The new Sandra?' says Sandra.

'She couldn't come for the first week,' says Belle, 'but she's here now.'

Angie, coming out of the lounge, says, 'Isn't it nice to have someone new?'

'But where's she going to sleep?' asks Sandra.

'In my room,' says Belle.

'But you're in a single room,' says Sandra.

'No, I'm in a twin,' says Belle.

'You ought to see it, Sandra,' says Angie. 'I don't like high ceilings myself because I like to be cosy, but it's a lovely room.'

While Angie goes into the kitchen to fetch more wine, Belle shepherds Sandra into the lounge. 'Here she is!' she says. 'Sandra, meet Sandra!'

The other Sandra is sitting on the two-seater sofa, smiling up at her. They exchange hellos.

'I bumped into her on my way back to pick up the picnic,' says Belle. 'She spent the afternoon with us.'

'We had great fun,' says Harriet. 'You didn't come.'

'No,' says Sandra. 'But I found another island, to the south of this one.'

'You mean Little Lieloh,' says Belle, 'where Valerie Swanson lived.'

'Little Lieloh?' says Sandra. 'I don't understand. I thought *this* was Valerie Swanson's house.'

'This is the old family home,' says Belle. 'Not that Valerie spent much time here. After her mother died, Valerie was sent away to boarding school on the mainland. She never finished school – she was discovered.' The word has possibilities – *doing what?* thinks Sandra, imagining something bad, imagining suspension or expulsion – and it takes her a moment to realise what Belle means. 'After some modelling, she went into the film industry.'

Belle makes it sound so easy, as if anyone could just step from one to the other, from school into films.

'It didn't last of course,' says Belle. 'She retired a few years later. She didn't return to the family home though; she got married, and then divorced, three times in all. She was very beautiful but impossible to live with. She had a notoriously bad temper.'

Angie chips in to describe with relish the biography's descriptions of Valerie's tantrums, during which she would veer between shutting herself in her room, slamming the door like a petulant child, and hurtling out, full of self-pitying rage. 'She could turn the air blue,' says Angie, 'and wasn't above throwing crockery when she didn't get her own way. Her divorces were brutal. However unbearable she was to live with, she could make life hell for anyone who tried to leave her.'

'Then her father died,' says Belle. 'Lieloh, along with the family home, was inherited by Valerie's twin brother, and Valerie got Little Lieloh. At one time, it was all one island, but at some point the southern peninsula became separated. Anyway, that's where Valerie built her house. She spent the rest of her life there.'

'She must have been happy there then,' says Sandra.

'No,' says Belle, 'I don't think she was. She'd inherited an island, but she'd wanted the bigger one. And she had enough money to build herself a house, that enormous house, but she was displeased with it. But however unhappy she was, however much she wanted her old world back, well, it had gone anyway.'

'I think she was a very lonely person,' says Angie.

'She must have been,' agrees Belle. 'The only family she had left was her brother, and there was no love lost between them.'

'She must have been popular though. There used to be boats all around the island. People came all the way out here wanting to see her,' says Sandra, who remembers her mother telling her this. 'She had parties,' she insists.

'Oh yes,' says Belle. 'I've been reading about these parties of hers. After spending months alone, she would throw an extravagant soirée.'

'*Feasting on society*,' quoted Angie, '*like a half-starved woman.*'

'Her Halloween parties were quite famous: grand costumes, the whole house decorated, jack-o'-lanterns along the path and at every window, the wine flowing, you know. But the only food she served to her guests was pumpkin pie. Does anyone *like* pumpkin pie?'

No one does.

'She made a big batch of them every year and no one ever ate them,' says Belle. 'She invited artists, writers, actors, though not young actresses, whom she loathed. She was always trying to cultivate her own creative set – or perhaps cultivate is not quite the right word . . . What is it you do to rhubarb? Yes, you force it. They went there willingly of course, out of curiosity, out of a kind of morbid fascination, and no doubt to meet and mix with other artists, although Valerie only invited the modestly talented, who would pose no threat to her own status. Her guests, discovering just how insufferable she was, never wanted to stay long, but she did her best to prolong their agony. And if, God forbid, she took a fancy to you, she would do her damnedest to keep you there. Apparently, the evening's pièce de résistance was Valerie singing music hall numbers and show tunes. In later years, no one was allowed to leave without enduring an interminable reading of her unpublished longform poetry, during which everyone was expected to be quiet and listen. I don't think anyone ever went twice. But she continued to send out invitations right up until she died last year. I don't know, by then, if anyone went.'

'I'd love to go,' says Sandra.

'It's out of bounds,' says Belle.

'Anyway,' says the other Sandra, 'we've got *this* island, haven't we?'

'We're very glad to have you here,' says Belle.

'You were ever so brave today,' says Harriet, 'jumping in off the rocks like that.'

'Oh yes,' agrees Angie. 'You're very daring.'

The other Sandra laughs. 'It was so cold! But that was half the fun!'

'You're a very strong swimmer,' says Belle.

'Oh yes,' says Alan. 'You beat us all in the races.'

Harriet shows some drawings of them all on the beach: nudes, which everyone admires.

'They're very clever,' says Belle.

'Yes,' says Angie. 'You have a real knack.'

Alan opens a bag of cheese and onion crisps just as Harriet turns to a picture of him eating a bag of cheese and onion crisps, and he chuckles.

'But you've none of Sandra,' says Angie.

'Yes I have,' says Harriet, showing Angie her sketches of the other Sandra.

'No, the other Sandra,' says Angie, pointing at Sandra.

'We can't both be called Sandra,' says Sandra. 'It will get confusing.'

It is suggested that they could use surnames, but being called 'Peters' would make Sandra feel as if she were in trouble, as if she were being summoned to the headmistress's office to be given detention.

'You can be Old Sandra and New Sandra,' suggests Angie.

'That's fine by me,' says New Sandra.

'I don't want to be Old Sandra,' says Sandra.

'Or, my friends call me Sandy.'

'We'll call you that then,' says Belle.

Sandra might have protested – her father calls her Sandy, and if either of them is going to be called Sandy she would have wanted it to be her – but she lets it go.

'Sandy paints landscapes,' says Angie, 'among other things. She was showing us some of her work. You ought to see it.' A display book is passed along, containing just the sort of thing Sandra tries for herself. She lingers over a beach scene, which she recognises – the sea turning to foam where it meets the headland, the family walking hand in hand beneath a heavy sky. This is not original work; this is a copy. Sandra says to the group, 'I've seen this before. It's from a magazine.'

'That's right,' says Sandy. 'I do a lot of magazine work.'

'Sandy's a freelance illustrator,' says Angie.

'Oh,' says Sandra, staring down at another glorious landscape.

'These aren't the originals, of course,' says Sandy. 'The originals are safe in my studio.'

There are God knows how many pages of this fine work, through which Sandra flips, muttering compliments, until finally she comes to the end and someone takes the book away from her.

She looks with annoyance at the chaos in the room: the Monopoly *still* has not been put away, nor the chess, and now the Twister mat is spread out on the floor. Some of the chess pieces have fallen over and when Sandra rights them, Sandy suggests a game. 'You and me,' she says, sitting forward.

While they make their moves, Alan tells them about two scientists who worked at a Soviet research station in Antarctica, near the Southern Pole of Inaccessibility. Angie says 'the Southern Pole of Inaccessibility' sounds like something from a children's story, like the Land of Far-Beyond.

'Or the Kingdom of Shadows,' suggests Sandra.

'That's not a children's book,' says Angie.

'I didn't say it was,' says Sandra.

'*The Land That Time Forgot*,' adds Harriet.

'Is that a children's book?' asks Sandra.

'It's a fantasy novel,' says Harriet, and Sandra pulls a face.

'They played one another at chess,' says Alan, 'and the one who lost was so enraged he attacked the other with an ice axe.'

'Charming,' says Angie.

It seems to Sandra, for most of the game, that she is going to win, but she suddenly sees she is bound to lose. Not caring to play out the final stages, to watch it happen, she resigns.

'There,' says Harriet, turning her pad around to show off the sketch she has been doing.

There is laughter, and Belle says, 'Oh dear . . .'

'I'm sorry, Sandra,' says Harriet, smiling.

'But you've captured her perfectly,' says Belle.

'Look at her face,' says Alan.

Sandra gets to her feet and goes to the door.

'Oh, don't sulk,' says Harriet.

'I'm not sulking,' says Sandra, shutting the door, leaving them to it. She goes into the kitchen, where Colin is washing up, and she asks, 'Is there something for me?'

'There was,' says Colin. 'But I threw it away.'

'It would have kept, wouldn't it,' says Sandra, 'in the oven, or the fridge?'

'I threw it out anyway,' says Colin. On the counter beside him is the Josephine Baker record, the smeared pieces that he has no doubt found in the bin, though she pushed them right down. She makes no acknowledgement, but goes to bed without her supper.

She should never have come here. It is not what she

imagined – she is in the wrong house, and her community of artists does not exist, or at least she is not a part of it. She pictures the others at the beach, naked and laughing, eating their lunch and running into the sea, Sandy being brave and beating them all.

With a sigh, Sandra gets into her bed, and turns from one side to the other, trying to get comfortable.

19

AFTER LIGHTING THE fire in her writing room, and sitting close enough to feel some warmth, Carol opens her laptop. To write, she has to silence the negative voice in her head telling her that this is no good, that she is wasting her time. *Give up*, says the voice. *Go home.* But she shushes it and presses on. She has passed the midway point and has a sense of the whole arc; it is just a question of having enough time to get it all down on the page. She believes that she must finish her novel here or not at all.

In this quiet room in this quiet house on this quiet island - disturbed by nothing more than the sound of the crackling fire and her own typing, and the wind and the rain and the sea and the incessant gulls - she can hardly imagine herself being back in the city. It is almost funny to think of herself hurrying along a busy street, with people all around her, with all that noise and all those choices.

It is not exactly idyllic here of course, but the sunsets are astonishing and at least the phone has been fixed. She has spoken to Jayne.

'Apparently,' said Jayne, 'your house was once owned by a film actress who'd gone into early retirement. I don't know who. This was after the war, so late forties. Who do you know of from those days? Judy Garland had a nervous breakdown around that time. Greta Garbo retired in the forties, very young. They were both Hollywood stars though, and I don't think yours was. And maybe she wasn't that big; she might have been some minor name we've never heard of.' She promised to do some research. 'And how are you?' she asked, in the same tone she would have used if Carol had been ill.

'I'm fine,' said Carol. 'Everything's fine.' She conceded that the house was *a little bit* creepy, and said she would be home soon, just as soon as she finished her novel.

It *can* be extremely irritating to be at the mercy of this temperamental old house in the back of beyond. Her computer, plugged in and with a full battery, has started switching itself off. The screen just goes black and she loses whatever she was in the middle of. Having to redo entire scenes is naturally slowing her down.

She no longer touches the piano. She was playing 'Chopsticks' – having reached the end, she was starting again – when the piano lid came crashing down. It almost crushed her hands, and with an injury like that she would not have been able to stay here typing. She would have had to leave, to seek medical attention; she would have had no choice.

Jayne still sends stories. Carol reads 'The Man Who Loved Islands', in which a man loses the will to write, and, at the same time, his lust for life itself; on his hump of rock, with the months going by, he ceases to care whether his writing is good or not and whether it is ever published, and at some point gives up working at his book at all.

Some evenings, Carol gets through a fair bit of the whisky that she now has delivered with her groceries. At least after that she sleeps well.

20

SANDRA HAS BEEN in bed for a long time, trying to ignore the noise and laughter coming from downstairs. Now she can hear them all coming to bed. When Angie lets herself into the darkened room, Sandra pretends she is sleeping. She tries not to breathe too loudly, not to sniff or clear her throat or swallow. Angie undresses quietly and slips into the bed by the window. When Angie whispers, 'Night night,' Sandra does not reply.

The idea comes to her both slowly – after tossing and turning while Angie snores – and quite suddenly: she will go to the bay by herself, right now; with no one there to see her, she will strip off and run naked over the sand and into the sea, or she will jump from the rocks. She will be brave.

She does not bother dressing. She creeps out onto the landing and down the stairs into the hallway, where she slips her feet into her walking boots and then quietly, stealthily, as if this were a break-in or an escape, she eases open the front door.

It is beautiful out there, beneath the stars. Some sit so low in the sky, grazing the horizon, that she can imagine herself just walking over there and touching them, although of course she could not. The moon is a sliver, like a sickle blade.

The island, at night, is so quiet, and bracingly cold. Sandra climbs over the stile and runs across the meadow, feeling, in her nightie, in the nighttime, like some kind of nymph.

When she reaches the bay she sheds her walking boots and her nightie, abandoning them in the sand as if they were fragments of something from which she is hatching and no longer needs. She walks to the shore and lets the sea run over her feet. It is bitterly cold. She inches forward, the icy water rising up her shins to her knees, up her thighs to her hips. Her shoulders are hunched, her hands clasped in front of her chest as if she were deep in prayer. She is trembling.

The way to do this is suddenly, to take that plunge from the rocks. She wades towards the dark heap of them. They are wet - the tide has been high but will be turning now - and slimy with seaweed; she will have to be careful not to slip. She finds a foothold and a handhold and begins to climb, spiderlike, edging out to where the sea is deeper. She was not expecting the sea to be so wild. She wonders what the hell she is doing here, naked at night on the rocks; she is no longer sure that she wants to jump, but she is here now, and she will do it.

She drops into the shatteringly cold water. When she emerges, shocked, gasping, getting her bearings, she is alarmed by how far she's been carried, and the distance she will have to swim to get back to dry land. She cannot go back to the rocks, against which she would break like the waves. She begins to swim, and how stupid, she thinks, how stupid to have done such a thing. She remembers being at the beach with Alex and Joe, the two of them working together to make a castle while Sandra went for a swim. She swam straight out, towards the horizon, out and out until finally she turned her head to look back at Alex and Joe and saw that they had gone. It was only when she tried to make her way back that she realised the tide was now against her. She was swimming as hard as she could but the distance to the shore did not seem to decrease. Her limbs were feeling soft, boneless, as in a dream. And all along, it was not they who had gone anywhere – they were right where she'd left them, building their sandcastle – it was she who had drifted so far that they were no longer in sight.

She stops, now, to feel with her toes for the seabed, but it is not there.

Stumbling finally into the shallows, standing unsteadily in the sand, weak and shivering, she might have been a creature newly birthed by the sea. Now she must go searching in the darkness for the things she left behind. She has forgotten to bring a towel.

Finally, in her sodden nightie, with her damp feet inside her unlaced boots, she makes her way back across the meadow. She wants to sneak into the house and go quietly to bed, to wake up in the morning as if none of this happened, as if it were nothing more than a dream, with only the salt and the sand that get everywhere to prove otherwise.

But though she enters as quietly as she can, someone upstairs has woken up, and is coming out of the shadows and down the stairs. 'Where have you been?' asks Angie.

Sandra, bedraggled and dripping in the hallway, underdressed and shuddering, feels like something unearthly trying to crawl into human society; she feels like an experiment gone wrong.

'I went to the bay,' she says. 'I went swimming.'

Belle calls down the stairs, 'Who's that?'

'It's me,' says Sandra.

'It's Sandra,' says Angie. 'She's been swimming.'

'In the middle of the night?' says Belle, coming down, snapping on the hallway light. She looks at Sandra in disbelief.

Others are emerging now, wanting to know what's going on.

'Sandra's been swimming,' says Belle.

'In the middle of the night?' says Harriet. 'Wasn't it cold?'

'Of course it was cold,' says Belle. She touches Sandra's bare arm. 'Freezing cold. You're like marble. And all alone in the middle of the night. Totally irresponsible.'

'Stupid.'

'But she didn't want to go,' says Harriet.

'She didn't want to go with *us*,' says Belle. 'You talk about a community,' she says to Sandra, 'but you don't even try to fit in. You drift along in your own little world.' She goes on, with the others joining in, but Sandra is no longer listening.

'I'm going to go to bed now,' she says, moving towards the stairs.

'Boots off, please,' says Belle.

Sandra takes off her boots. Someone turns out the hallway light and Sandra climbs the stairs. Her legs are heavy and weak and do not feel like her own. She hears Sandy, up on the landing in the dark, saying, *I've got a spare nightie she can wear, and I'll give her my blanket*, and someone else says warmly, *You are good, Sandy.*

21

JAYNE SENDS A picture of Greta Garbo, and at the bottom she has written I *want to be alone!* There is a spare frame in the hallway cupboard that fits it perfectly, and there is a toolbox. Carol hammers a hook into the wall above her bed and hangs the picture on it.

That same night she is woken by something sharp striking her forehead. She thinks she has been attacked but when she looks she can see, in the weak light of dawn, she's alone. She turns on the lamp and sees the picture on her pillow, the shards of glass – perhaps it hit the headboard, she thinks, as it fell. There is a hole in the wall where the hook was. Either she did a bad job or else the walls are crumbling. There is a wound on her forehead but it is not too bad.

Carefully, she gets up. She moves the picture in its broken frame onto the bedside table, then takes the pillow to the wastepaper basket, tips in the broken glass, and peels off the pillowcase. It is still very early and she would like to go back to sleep. She considers the other bedrooms but decides against them, preferring to remain in her own room. She inspects the sheet for nasty sparkles before lying down again, thinking vaguely about head wounds and the dangers of falling asleep.

When she wakes again, it is with a peculiar feeling that there is someone in the house. Lying still, she hears voices. They are downstairs: she can hear Roman, and strangers, laughing and clinking glasses, as if they were having a party.

Since the phone's been fixed, Roman has generally called ahead, but sometimes he can't; sometimes Carol finds that the phone cable has come out of the wall. Roman turns up with picnics, to check that all is well. He rarely comes into the house and never stays long or late or overnight. Carol thought at first that he was being gentlemanly, not wanting to impose. Now she knows how he dislikes this place.

She sits up, pushing away her covers, sorry to lose her warmth. She puts her bare feet on the floor and listens. She can hear him on the stairs now, and before she can move one way or the other he is entering, bringing the strangers into her room, intruding while her head is still thick with sleep, while she is still in her nightclothes.

'Carol!' says Roman, as if surprised she is not yet up and about - though that must already have been apparent - or as if surprised to find her there at all, as if he had forgotten she existed, while Carol is offended by what strikes her as trespass into what she has started to think of as her house. 'I've brought Mr and Mrs Piggott to look around,' he tells her. 'They're considering buying.'

'We are considering,' confirms Mr Piggott.

'This,' says Roman, gesturing towards his houseguest, 'is Carol Clark. Carol's an author!'

'Are you really?' says Mrs Piggott, studying Carol. 'I haven't heard of you.' She turns to her husband. 'Have you heard of Carol Clark?' He hasn't heard of her either. Mrs Piggott turns back to Carol and asks what she has written.

'Mostly short stories,' says Carol.

'I don't like short stories,' says Mrs Piggott.

'But she's working on a novel,' says Roman.

'Oh yes?' says Mrs Piggott.

'A fantasy novel,' adds Roman.

'Oh, that's not my sort of thing,' says Mrs Piggott.

'You're quite at home here, aren't you, Carol?' asks Roman. Carol thinks at first that he is mocking her dishevelment – her personal appearance and the state of her room. But she sees from the strain on his face that he is just keen to assure the potential buyers that this house can be a home, that it can be lived in.

'Oh yes,' she agrees, 'I'm very much at home here.'

Roman looks delighted, because if she is at home here, Mr and Mrs Piggott are more likely to buy, and then Carol will have to leave.

'We won't keep you,' says Roman, ushering Mr and Mrs Piggott out into the hallway.

'An author!' says Mrs Piggott in hushed tones to her husband, as the door closes on Carol, still perched on the edge of her mattress, half in and half out of her untidy bed, with her face unwashed, her hair unbrushed, in her nightie with no underwear on.

She won't be able to write a word while there are people in the house. They spend what seems to Carol like an eternity in the hallway, going in and out of rooms until they must have seen everything there is to see many times over. And all the while, Carol knows, Roman will be itching to get away.

Even after they've gone, the sense of disturbance remains. Carol washes her bedding, mindful of glass – slivers invisible to her naked eye – that might get stuck in the palms of her hands or in her fingertips. She finds an acceptable frame and rehangs the picture of Greta Garbo. When the hook comes out again, she tries a different wall, and when it comes out again, she gives up.

22

SANDRA WAKES FEELING odd, fuzzy, as if she were ill. Her silk dress looms like a headless lady at the end of the bed. The curtains are still drawn but she sees from her clock that it is very late, almost lunchtime. She gets up carefully, feeling strange in the borrowed nightie, which is slightly too small at the neck and slightly too short in the arms. She looks for her own nightie, which is presumably lying around somewhere, damp and salty like something beached, but she cannot find it. It will need washing and drying.

She takes a shower and dresses warmly in her fleece. Downstairs, she eats breakfast, which is also lunch. She has wasted a whole morning, while everyone else is out there, working. But at least today, for once, she thinks – as she puts on her coat and her slightly damp boots, picks up her satchel and leaves the house – she knows where she is going.

The sun has already passed its peak as Sandra walks south along the dirt track, past the first turn-off where her sea turned to concrete, past the second turn-off where she lost her horizon, past the third turn-off to the disappointing chapel. She comes to the top of the incline and the edge of the copse beyond which is the stretch of grass in which she was expecting to sit, to get down to work, but there is Sandy, sitting on a special artist's stool, painting Little Lieloh.

Sandy senses her presence, glances over her shoulder and smiles.

'You're painting the island,' says Sandra.

'Yes,' says Sandy.

Sandra moves closer, to see how she's doing. Even as a work in progress, Sandy's Little Lieloh has a depth and life and charm that Sandra, before she has even started, knows her own will lack. 'How do you do that?' she asks.

'Do what?' asks Sandy.

Sandra gestures to her painting.

'It's just a question of technique,' says Sandy. Indicating the little island beyond them, she talks about, for example, the sense of distance, about warmth in the foreground versus a comparative coolness of colour and loss of definition further out, further back. Sandra tries to pay attention, but she is distracted by Sandy's mirrored sunglasses, in which she can see herself reflected back, squinting.

She will come back tomorrow, she decides, when she can have the whole day and the place to herself. 'I'll leave you to it,' she tells Sandy, walking on, away from where she wanted to be, keeping to the south end of the island but moving out of sight of Little Lieloh.

She picks some wild flowers which are unlike anything she has seen before, and spends the afternoon diligently sketching each one.

Back at the house, pausing in the hallway, she thinks for a moment that someone has found another record to play, before realising that what she can hear is Sandy singing in the kitchen while she prepares their evening meal. The others, judging by their chatter, seem to be in the lounge.

Sandra heads upstairs to attend to her scrapbook. The flowers she has already pressed can now be taped in next to the corresponding pictures. It's not so easy to match them up now they're dried out and flattened, but all in all she is pleased with the look of the pages. The flowers she picked today have travelled well, they are almost undamaged, and she arranges them for pressing. When she has done that, she takes off her painting clothes, putting them aside to wash with her nightie. Lifting down her dress, she discovers a rip in it, a long rip in the skirt. If it was there when she last wore it, or when she hung it up, she did not notice. She has a travel sewing kit somewhere but already she can hear Sandy banging on the saucepan, calling everyone through. She will have to put up with the rip for now, she thinks, putting the dress on anyway, hoping not to make things worse.

The others have gathered around the kitchen table, wanting to know what's for dinner. 'It certainly smells good,' says Belle.

Sandy lifts a dish out of the oven and brings it to the table. 'I've made a lasagne,' she says.

'Oh, I like a decent lasagne,' says Angie.

Sandra takes her place.

'And I've made you a cheese salad,' says Sandy, 'with Stilton and walnuts.'

'Oh, you are good, Sandy,' says Angie.

Sandra, smoothing down her dress, accepts her salad.

When everyone is seated, Sandy says, 'Shall I say grace?'

'Oh yes, please do,' says Belle.

Putting her hands together and bowing her head, Sandy says, 'We give You thanks for food and drink and all that You provide: flowers, mountains, stars above, family by our side. Grant that we might hear Your voice and always be our Guide; from now until the end of time may we, in You, abide. Amen.'

'That was really lovely,' says Alan, smiling at Sandy, who smiles back.

'A poem!' says Angie. 'That was beautiful, Sandy.'

Sandra picks at her salad. It is not easy to get a walnut

and a lettuce leaf onto the end of a fork. She washes her meal down with more wine than she is used to, with very little to soak it up. It will leave her feeling sullen and tired. Meanwhile, the others clean their plates and ask for seconds.

When it is time for dessert, Colin volunteers to fetch the ice cream from the cellar. Belle suggests someone else ought to go because he fetched it yesterday, and the day before. 'I don't mind,' says Colin, who is already on his way. No one insists: the cellar is rather grim – claustrophobic and cobwebby – and they are only too glad to have a volunteer. 'You might as well bring up some bottles of wine while you're at it,' calls Belle.

After their ice cream, they take their wine through to the lounge, where Sandy shows off her first full day's work. Her picture of Little Lieloh is very good, and the others say so. There is a sense of light in the sky, a sense of motion in the water. It is better than anything Sandra has ever done.

'I'm quite pleased with my sketches,' says Sandra. She fetches her scrapbook and shows the group the wild flowers she's done, including the earlier ones with the actual flowers attached as evidence.

'Did you pick them here?' asks Belle.

'Yes,' says Sandra. 'There were lots I'd never seen before.'

'You shouldn't pick them,' says Belle. 'You should leave them to grow.'

Angie leans over to have a look. 'They are beautiful,' she says. 'You should have left them alone.'

Sandy asks Angie about her poetry.

'I'm trying to express everything in haiku,' says Angie. She has made a good start, she says, and reads a selection, while Sandra sits and drinks her wine until eventually Angie stops talking. Sandy touches Angie's arm and says all the right things.

Alan comes through from the kitchen. Now, thinks Sandra, they'll get out more games, and she does not want to play. She says, 'I need to find my nightie.'

'It had to be thrown out,' says Belle. 'Didn't it, Colin?'

'Well, it was ruined, Belle,' says Colin.

'Thrown out?' says Sandra.

'Seawater rots clothing,' says Belle.

'Not *instantly*,' says Sandra.

'You can keep my old one,' says Sandy.

'You ought to have rinsed it out last night,' says Belle.

'I can rinse it out now,' says Sandra. 'It will still be salvageable.'

'I doubt it,' says Belle. 'It went in the bin with yesterday's leftovers.'

'And today's,' adds Alan.

Sandra leaves the room (*in a huff*, she hears someone say) and goes into the kitchen, where she picks through the waste until she finds her nightie, stained and damaged. She pushes it back down and goes up to bed.

In the bathroom, she thinks about bleach; she thinks about very clever stitching, which she cannot do, and new lace, but she does not, in the end, go back for it. She puts on the borrowed nightie, and pulls at the neck, which seems to be shrinking. She gets into her bed and tries to sleep.

23

CAROL OPENS HER eyes. She knows she heard something, a noise downstairs. Her first thought is Roman, who has his own key, who will tidy the kitchen and dress it with flowers, or who is bringing people who will want to buy Little Lieloh, who will want this house for themselves, who will want her gone. It is still nighttime though; Roman might be an early bird but there's barely a hint of light yet. So then she thinks of burglars – imagining strangers with crowbars, a kicked-in door, a broken window – though she doubts they'd go to the trouble of coming here.

She wraps herself in her dressing gown, goes very quietly onto the landing and listens. 'Hello?' she calls. Hearing nothing now, she sneaks downstairs. Cautiously, she checks the reception rooms, and looks in the kitchen. There is no one there, as far as she can see. There is nothing but moonlight and her own mess. She can imagine the big window framing something alarming – that burglar, still trying to break in, or some sinister fantasy creature straight out of her imagination – but there is only darkness. Moving closer, she feels the cold coming in through the glass. She looks out at the sea, at the moonlight gleaming off it, at the horizon heavy with stars, like the hem of a ballgown weighed down by its own decorative jewels. She likes this image and writes it down on a scrap of paper.

Upstairs, she looks into a few of the bedrooms, and then,

though she has not opened every door, has not gone right to the far end of the corridor, and could not swear on her life there is nobody there, she decides it was nothing, perhaps just a dream, and goes back to bed.

When she wakes in the morning and goes through the house again in the daylight, it does look undisturbed, except, in the kitchen, next to the sink, she finds a note. Roman, she thinks; he has been here after all. She picks up the note and reads it: *the horizon heavy with stars, like the hem of a ballgown weighed down by its own decorative jewels.* The only person sneaking around this house last night – the only elf leaving questionable gifts on her worktop – was herself.

That garlicky smell is downstairs now. Carol opens the kitchen window to let it out, though at the same time she thinks that might make the smell worse because it must be coming from the wild garlic that grows outside. The breeze is nice though, and it does somehow alleviate the worst of that overpowering smell. When the window slides back down, Carol pushes it up again. While she is looking for something with which to wedge it, the window slams down, and the crackle glaze vase smashes, and Carol decides to keep the window closed.

24

THEY ARE ALL in the hallway, lacing their boots and zipping their coats.

'The weather's really turned now,' says Sandy, pulling on bright pink gloves.

Sandra stares. 'Those are my gloves,' she says.

'These are my gloves,' says Sandy. 'They go with my coat.'

'But I've lost some just like that,' says Sandra. 'Did you find them here?'

'Have they got your name in?' asks Belle.

'No,' says Sandra. 'But mine look just like that.'

'Just leave it,' says Belle, as if this were some dirty brawl and someone were about to get hurt.

'I just want to know if you found them here,' says Sandra, but Sandy's already at the door and walking away with Belle while Sandra's still in her socks.

When Sandra has her boots on and something for lunch in her satchel, she heads out into the insipid morning light. She walks south, pleased there is no one in sight.

Beyond the copse, but still well back from the danger sign, she settles cross-legged in the deep grass, among mushrooms or toadstools or whatever they are.

She imagines swimming over to the island. She is not good at judging distances but it can't be more than half a mile, not much more than she could manage. But it's no good getting *most* of the way, she tells herself: she might sink and no one would even know. She would need to get back as well.

She gets out her watercolour pad, opens her tin of paints and looks at the cloudless blue sky, the darker sea, and the island in the near distance, the white house, its front door warmed by the rising sun, whose light glints off the windows.

She spends the morning trying to get the view onto the page, but it just looks ridiculous. It doesn't look real. The palm trees at the edge of the island make it look like a fantasy of the kind of island on which one might be shipwrecked, in rags, a message in a bottle washing up on the shore.

By the time the sun peaks, Sandra has given up and is eating her lunch, keeping her macaroni cheese pie and her tipsy cake close, watching for gulls.

She decides to spend the afternoon focusing on the house itself. With her pad on her lap and her pencil in her hand, she sits and eyes the structure. She ought to have brought binoculars, for the details. She sets about making her pencil marks, expecting the hard, straight lines to be easier than the evasive landscape, and then finding that's not the case. She has to keep rubbing out and starting again, and when her rubber tears the thinning paper, or when her ugly lines are too deep to rub out, she turns the page and starts again, but still she cannot get it right. It looks like a dollhouse; it is too far away.

In the end, she packs up without finishing, not at all happy with what she has, but at least she has tried. She waits to watch the sun go down. It looks like a little golden island sinking into the sea, and then it is gone.

She returns to the house just as the others are going into the kitchen. There is a strong smell in the hallway. 'Is that fish?' asks Sandra.

'Of course,' says Belle, 'fish on Friday,' as if that's the rule and Sandra ought to obey. 'Alan caught it.'

Sandra, following Belle into the kitchen, says to Alan, 'You caught your own fish?' She can see he caught plenty.

Alan, glancing up, says, 'I didn't make anything for you.'

'I'm not hungry anyway,' says Sandra, though she's starving. She sits down and pours herself a glass of wine. There are potatoes to go with the fish, so Sandra eats those, and thinks of *The Potato Eaters*, van Gogh's coarse-faced, bony-handed peasants who have unearthed their own potatoes, who would catch their own fish. Sandra used to fish in the stream at the end of her parents' garden. She never caught a thing with that rod which was only a stick, the line just a piece of string with a paperclip hook on the end but no bait. She spent hours there though, with nobody seeming to worry where she was or what she was doing. She had a lot of freedom, and took it for granted. It was idyllic really. They're stricter with Joe.

Sandra's dinner of potatoes and vanilla ice cream almost leaves her yearning for a cheese salad. While Colin returns the ice cream tub to the freezer, the others take their wine glasses into the lounge.

Angie says she's got some poetry she's been working on for a week and she still isn't sure if it's finished.

'It can be really hard to know,' says Sandra. 'When I had my exhibition—'

'Let Angie finish,' says Belle. The others encourage Angie to read out her work, so Angie, in her nasal voice, reads a poem that is terribly long, or perhaps it is more than one poem and Sandra missed the point at which one ended and another began.

While Angie is thanking them all for listening, Colin comes in with the brown paper bags. They are passed around, and there are some comments about how much they've got through.

'They only came on Wednesday,' says Alan.

'Have we all been sleepwalking?' asks Belle. 'Have we been eating them in our sleep?'

Sandra finishes her wine and announces she's going to bed.

'Night night,' says Sandy, who looks very comfortable, with a caramel cream puff in one hand and the Angela Carter in the other, spreading out into the space that Sandra has left, getting her feet up onto the cushion, which will still be warm.

25

CAROL FINDS HERSELF checking the doors and the windows at bedtime, even though the noise in the night wasn't burglars, and even though, if burglars came, they could come at any time.

If she's honest with herself, Carol has started to think there might be *something* in the house.

'Something?' asks Jayne, when Carol tells her this. Jayne's voice, over the phone, always sounds kind of distant.

'A presence,' says Carol. 'A spiritual presence.'

Of course, she thinks, that's why the film students changed their minds about staying here; that's why they cut their trip short. It's why no one wants the house, why it stands empty. *Or not so empty!* She thinks she might, once she's home, pitch an article for *Supernatural Magazine*.

Jayne asks how much longer Carol is going to stay on Little Lieloh, but Carol doesn't know. Whenever Jayne asks when she's coming home, Carol says, 'Soon.' She has been saying that for months.

Carol calls Roman to ask if the house might be haunted.

'Haunted?' says Roman. He sounds concerned. 'What makes you say that?'

Carol feels suddenly foolish: anything she might say sounds so insubstantial. 'Just noises in the night,' she says. 'I got spooked.'

'You're all right?' asks Roman.

'Oh yes, I'm fine,' says Carol. In fact, she feels rather pleased with herself that if the house has a ghost, she isn't terribly scared of it; if the house has a ghost, it feels like a welcoming one. She cannot imagine how she could keep living here if the ghost did not like her.

Carol asks about the previous occupant.

'The man I bought the house from didn't live in it,' says Roman. 'But I believe its previous owner lived there until the day she died.'

Carol wants to know how she died, and Roman protests that things are taking a rather morbid turn but he tells her the lady died of old age, in her own bed, during the night. All alone, he concedes, but it would have been a peaceful sort of death. Carol is glad of that because a peaceful death ought to mean a peaceful ghost.

She has decided that the bedroom at the far end of the upstairs hallway, the insanely ostentatious one, belongs to the ghost. She never goes in there without knocking now, and rarely goes in at all. But from time to time, when in the mood, the ghost comes out.

Carol has a feeling that the ghost does not like it when she leaves the windows open, so she is sure to keep everything closed. And it does not like her banging in nails, hanging pictures, trying to make the place her own.

Guessing from the record sleeves that the ghost likes jazz, she says to it, 'I like jazz too!' and asks Jayne to send some Miles Davis and Duke Ellington, Billie Holiday and Josephine Baker. Jayne sends CDs, which Carol plays on her laptop until, one by one, they go missing. 'Not to your liking?' she asks. Eyeing the piano, untouched since the lid nearly took her fingers off, Carol says, 'And you didn't like my piano playing, did you? Well, that's all right. No offence taken!' She laughs, and then stops because it sounds creepy when she's there on her own. *Or not!*

When noises wake her in the night, she calls out gaily, 'Would you mind keeping it down?!' Of course, she tells herself, most likely it *isn't* a ghost; most likely it's just this old house settling and she's just being foolish. She puts a pillow over her head and goes back to sleep. In the morning, she finds the pretty room with the picture window has been smashed up.

26

SANDRA GOES INTO the bathroom, where Angie's wet towel has been left on the floor. It infuriates her.

In the shower, she uses a small amount of Sandy's fancy products, including the last of a micro exfoliating balm.

She still has not washed her painting clothes. She keeps putting them aside for the purpose and then retrieving them unwashed. Tonight, when she gets in, when she changes for dinner, she will wash them in the sink; she is looking forward to wearing clean clothes. Angie's handwashing is always draped around the bedroom, around the whole damn house, over the banisters and the backs of chairs.

When Sandra is dressed, she takes her satchel and goes downstairs. Finding herself alone in the kitchen, she looks for the bakery items. As well as breakfast, she will need a packed lunch. She cannot find them though; they must have been finished last night, or else the bags have been hidden.

'Are you looking for something, Sandra?' asks Alan, appearing suddenly in the doorway.

'Just something to keep me going,' says Sandra, reaching for a banana. Glancing outside, she sees Colin, Belle and Sandy at the picnic table. She does not want to join them. She goes into the hallway and puts the banana into her satchel.

Harriet, coming in from the garden, says to Sandra, 'You're leaving early.'

'I wanted to make a start,' says Sandra. She puts on her

boots and her coat. She just wants to get out of this house now.

She walks to the south end of the island, where once again she sits down in the grass, facing the smaller island and its curious house, and gets out her pad and pencil and paints.

She cannot, however carefully she tries, however steady she keeps her hand, get her horizon right. When she draws freehand, it is not flat enough; when she uses a ruler, it is *too* flat. The sky is interesting – the layers of cloud and the way the light is trying to push through – but she cannot get it right.

The sea seems darker than before. She is mixing shades when she hears people, and recognises Belle's foghorn of a voice. Anticipating someone at her shoulder, peering at her work, she turns the page. The sound of people recedes.

Sandra puts down her work and eats her banana and wishes she had more.

Abandoning her first attempt, she spends the afternoon having another go at the horizon, the inky sea, and the clouds with the light behind them.

'If you stay here much longer,' says Belle, somewhere behind her, 'you'll put down roots.' Sandra turns to see her walking away, flanked by the terrible clash of Harriet's orange and Sandy's pink.

It is no good anyway. She packs up, ready to get back to the house. She is thirsty, but she has used all her water for painting; she has turned it all blue and poured it away.

Despite the little danger sign, Sandra cannot resist sidling up to the edge to take a look over, and is rewarded not only by the sight of a little bay down below but a flight of steps set into the cliff wall. Cautiously, wanting a handrail, she descends. Of course, the narrow shingle beach does not bring her significantly closer to the little island, and the view from here is much the same, but at least she has come as far as she can, she thinks, casting her eye over this desolate shore, the shingle in shadow, the crumbling cliff edge, a single stunted tree, tied to which is a rowing boat. She has been in rowing boats with Alex and Joe, on boating lakes where there was always an island, towards which they would head, before circling it, never getting too close, and rowing back.

The boat is protected by a tarpaulin, beneath which it seems to be intact, with the oars stowed in the hull, ready and waiting. Sandra amuses herself with the idea of taking this boat and setting out to sea, going north, rowing for mile after mile until she is home. Really, even imagining covering such a distance is difficult, whereas this little stretch of water to the south, lying between her and Little Lieloh, does seem doable. With the place to herself, with no one looming over her shoulder, no one looking at what she is doing and making negative comments, she could be perfectly happy.

The light is going from the sky. She really ought to be getting back. But tomorrow, she thinks, tomorrow.

Through the kitchen window, she can see Colin making dinner. He sees her too, and turns away. He is no longer speaking to her, she has noticed. If she passes him on the landing, in the hallway, on the stairs, and even if she speaks to him, he acts as if she isn't there. She finds the silence surprisingly aggressive, and childish: it is like being back at school and sent to Coventry.

She doesn't care though. She has her island and a rowing boat to get her there. She goes upstairs and straight into the bathroom where she strips off her painting clothes and washes them in the sink, thinking how nice it will be to feel fresh. Out on the landing, she makes space between Angie's damp maternity clothes and hangs her things over the banisters to dry.

She goes into the bedroom. The rip in her dress looks even worse now. She locates her travel sewing kit, which is rather basic, from a Christmas cracker, but it will do the job until she can get home. None of the threads in the kit is the right colour, but she chooses one anyway and threads her needle and has just put a knot in the end when she hears the clatter of the spoon inside the saucepan telling her it is time to go down. Even though she is acutely aware of this ugly tear in her special dress, she doubts it would be very obvious to anyone else. She puts it on and checks her image in the mirror. She will have to do. She goes down, to join the others who are now in the kitchen, and finds there is nothing for her.

While Colin says grace, Sandra, without comment, sets about making herself a cheese sandwich, which she sits and eats without giving thanks, washing it down with the Swansons' apparently endless, run-of-the-mill wine.

After dessert, they take their seats in the lounge. Belle tops up their wine glasses and Sandy passes round a page torn from a glossy magazine, a picture of a celebrity with good hair. 'Do you think I could carry that off?' she asks.

Everyone agrees the hairstyle would suit her very well.

'I'd have that done myself,' says Sandra.

'It wouldn't work on you, Sandra,' says Belle. 'Your face is the wrong shape.'

When Angie comes through from the kitchen, she takes up her knitting, her baby's cardigan, which is almost finished: she just has the little buttons to sew on. She gets out some matching yarn and a needle.

Alan peels off a sock and shows Angie the hole in the heel. 'That could do with sewing up,' he says.

'A stitch in time,' says Angie.

He borrows a needle and thread and puts on his reading glasses.

'I ought to mend the hole in my coat pocket,' says Belle.

'I have some sewing to do too,' says Sandra. She can mend the rip in her dress without taking it off, sewing herself into it, as it were. Sewing is a task that she always puts off, and yet, when she gets down to it, she finds it very peaceful and satisfying. In fact, she made a brief foray into textile art. 'When I had my exhibition,' she says, 'it included some textile work that I think came out quite well.' In fact, she can show them: one of the pieces is upstairs, being used as a bookmark. She goes up to her room to fetch her needle and thread and the textile bookmark of which she is rather proud. She is bemused by the thought of them all sitting there doing their mending together, like members of a sewing circle. Returning to the lounge, she walks in on laughter. Colin is wrapped in one of the flowery curtains, saying in a self-satisfied voice, 'When I had my exhibition . . .' Sandra stands in the doorway, with the bookmark she wanted to show them crushed in her hand, the Christmas-cracker travel-kit needle piercing her finger. She turns away, the blood draining from her face as she crosses the hallway. She can hear them stifling their laughter; someone lets out a snort. She hears Sandy saying, 'You should go and apologise,' but no one comes after her.

In the bathroom, she brushes her teeth, scrubbing as if she were trying to take off the enamel, and washes her face so furiously she might have been trying to rub it off, wash it away. She would comb her hair but she believes her comb has been borrowed, by Angie, and never returned.

She goes, with her autumn-pale face and her sea-breeze-tangled hair, into her room. She does not want to change into

Sandy's uncomfortable nightie; she will not wear Sandy's cast-offs any more. In fact, she need not change at all: this tired old silk dress can be her nightgown. She gets into bed, picks up her book to help her settle, and finds she has lost her place.

27

WHEN CAROL TELLS Roman what happened in the night, what she found in the morning, he does not seem overly surprised. He asks her if she is all right.

'I'm not hurt,' says Carol. 'I'm just a bit shaken up.'

'Which room was it?' asks Roman.

'The pretty room with the picture window,' says Carol.

'Oh yes,' says Roman.

It's not so pretty now, what with the broken mirror and the broken ornaments and the broken furniture.

'It probably looks worse than it is,' says Roman. He is quiet for a moment, though she can hear that he's still there on the end of the line. 'Perhaps I should come and fetch you,' he suggests.

'Just give me a little bit longer,' says Carol.

After speaking with Roman, Carol calls Jayne and tells her what the ghost has done this time. 'Carol,' says Jayne gently, 'I really think you should come home.'

'I will,' says Carol, 'soon. Don't worry about the ghost.'

'I'm not worried about the ghost,' says Jayne. 'I'm worried about you.'

Carol insists that she has never been harmed here, apart from the wound inflicted by the picture frame, which might have been an accident. The incident with the piano lid was a close shave but it didn't actually touch her. On the whole, the ghost seems to like her.

Nonetheless, Carol sleeps badly that night. She isn't sure she has slept at all. Before it is quite light, she opens the curtains, as if that might make the day start. The sky is streaked with red. She gets back into bed and reads a children's novel, *Moominpappa at Sea*, whose loneliness and strangeness leave her more unsettled than before.

By the time she gets up, it is raining, heavily enough to stop her going for her usual morning circuit of the island. If she works first, she thinks, she can go out at lunchtime, but she finds herself stuck and distracted, and at lunchtime it is still raining. This weather is making her feel cooped up, which puts her in a bad mood.

Even at the end of the afternoon, the rain is showing no sign of stopping, but it is slacker now, a constant drizzle. Carol decides to put on the wellies that live in the hallway cupboard and go outside. Without fresh air and exercise she fears another restless night. Besides, she almost forgot, today's a delivery day.

From the top of the path that leads to the jetty, she sees the waterproof box, her groceries dutifully left on the shore, as if there were some monster on this island needing offerings to appease it, or as if there were plague victims here. She collects the box gratefully and carries it back towards the house, past the privet shrubs which crowd the path so badly now that she has to push her way through. In the half-light, the house, so starkly white, has a kind of glow; it looks almost unreal, phantasmagoric.

The ferryman never forgets her, even in foul weather like this, or especially in foul weather like this. When Carol unpacks her groceries in the kitchen, she finds he has put in some extras: a pair of hand-knitted socks and a tub of home-made soup.

And there's a letter from Jayne, which includes some information she's dug up about the neighbouring island of Lieloh, the Swansons who once lived there, and a descendant who developed the place as an artists' retreat – *an ambition that was nearly scuppered by some sort of accident,* writes Jayne. *Apparently someone was found dead in a cellar.* How awful, thinks Carol. There are no further details. She supposes, in that sort of environment, there can be personality clashes, moments of tension; she thinks of the cabin fever of *Big Brother,* and the recent news report of a scientist at an Antarctic outpost stabbing a colleague who kept telling him the endings of books.

And the old film actress whose home you're in, adds Jayne, *was Valerie Swanson. After she retired, she built that house on Little Lieloh and lived there until she died about twenty years ago. Ever heard of her? No entry on Wikipedia. So no one exciting, I'm afraid!*

No one exciting is fine by Carol. She puts on the socks that the ferryman sent her, and makes a cup of hot chocolate. She is tired, ready to drop, but still she stays up for as long as she can, and leaves the lamp on while she sleeps.

28

SANDRA HEARS THE creak of bed springs. Opening her eyes, she sees Angie stirring, and squints at her clock. It is time to get up, but she closes her eyes for a moment and goes back to sleep.

By the time she wakes again, she's alone. Angie's bed is empty, her bedding slumping to the floor. It is almost nine o'clock. There is no coming and going on the landing, and no one in the bathroom.

She can see from the stairs that there is no one in the hallway. Someone has been busy making chains of paper dolls, though closer up she sees they are not the smiling dolls she used to make: they are skeletons, clinging to one another's skeletal hands, and ghosts, not holding one another at all, just touching at the edges. She has lost track of the days, but it is, she realises now, the end of the month; they have made the house ready for Halloween.

The paper dolls are everywhere, strung across the ceilings and the doorframes so that Sandra has to duck her head at the foot of the stairs, and again to get into the kitchen. The house is strangely silent. She can see through the window that there's no one in the garden. She goes back into the hallway, ripping down the blasted decorations that keep getting in her face. She doesn't see why they're there: it's not as if there will be trick or treaters coming to the door this evening. She just hopes no one's planning a party.

There is no one in the lounge. The house is deserted; everyone's gone, leaving only traces of themselves: their tea and coffee mugs, their crumby plates, their empty coat pegs. She feels like Rip Van Winkle, who slept for longer than he meant to; he returned home to find his world unrecognisable and that he had all but been forgotten.

She wants a shower, but the ferry will come today and she does not want to be oblivious beneath the lukewarm drizzle if the man comes early again: she wants her letter to go and to place her order. She could leave a note on the table but she does not trust that it would be seen or obeyed, so she waits. She has a leisurely breakfast, enjoying the last of the eggs, and then goes upstairs to fetch the letter, as well as some work to be getting on with. She finds a note from Angie on the chest of drawers: *We're going to watch the sun rise.* There is an invitation to join them, but it's too late now.

Sandra makes herself comfortable in the lounge, on the three-seater sofa, from which the front path is visible. Harriet has left behind one of her sketchpads, inside which is that hateful sketch from the other night. Sandra tears herself out, tears herself up, throws the pieces away. She spends some time sticking her pressed flowers into her scrapbook, then flips through the pages with a critical eye. The work she has done is a million miles from what's in that book on the shelf, and it's not even what she is here for.

By one o'clock, Sandra is at the window, thinking the man will surely arrive at any moment, but the minutes tick by and still no one comes. She adds up the time it will take her to walk to the south shore, to row to the island, to have enough time there to make it worthwhile, and get back before it gets dark. She is hungry again, and drifts through to the kitchen. She finds some leftovers to have for her lunch, and decides she will have wine as well, and dessert: in the absence of cakes and pastries, she goes down to the cellar for ice cream. They've been eating ice cream for days but there are still half a dozen tubs in the freezer. She takes one that's been opened, and which feels almost empty, and brings it up, but when she takes off the lid, instead of ice cream she finds a bird at the bottom of the washed-out tub. It is sparrow-like, greyish-brown, quite dead of course. With a cry of disgust, she pushes it away. It is no doubt one of Colin's found objects, which he wants to preserve; he will want to keep it at home in a morbid diorama.

And what about the other tubs? she wonders. Some are no doubt full of ice cream, but she is grimly curious. She returns to the cellar, looks in the chest freezer and finds another tub that's been opened, which contains a small mammal. It is horrible, truly horrible, having all these dead things in the house; it is untenable. There are other tubs in the freezer but she does not want to open them, and has lost her appetite.

Besides, returning to the kitchen, she sees it is now two o'clock, and she thinks perhaps the ferry will not come after all. She thinks about the rowing boat that is waiting to take her to Little Lieloh. She worries that she is running out of time. Just as she is getting to her feet, she sees the buggy coming to a stop outside the house, and there is the man lifting out the deliveries.

Sandra meets him in the hallway. 'You're late today,' she says, as if she were the lady of the house chiding the grocer's boy.

'I'm not late,' he says.

Sandra shows him the time.

He sets down his load and opens the fridge, and tells her the clocks have gone back.

Of course. It's the last Sunday in October. She dislikes

these days when the clocks change: it makes time feel weirdly fluid, and it takes her a while to adjust, but she is pleased to have regained a valuable hour.

'Are you not out doing your art today?' says the man, making space on the untidy table for half a dozen fat brown paper bags.

'I wanted to see you first,' says Sandra. 'I have something that needs posting.' She hands him her letter, and he puts it into his pocket, saying he will post it from Liel first thing in the morning.

'How are you finding the house?' he asks.

'It's all right,' says Sandra. 'It does get cold.'

'It does,' agrees the man.

'And you might ask the owner to consider getting a washer dryer.'

'I'm the owner,' says the man.

'You own the house?' says Sandra.

'I own this whole place,' he says. 'I inherited it from the old man earlier this year.'

Sandra, looking more closely at him now, says, 'You're a Swanson?' She is surprised, as if she might have expected to recognise one on sight.

The man gathers up his empty boxes.

'It's quite an inheritance,' says Sandra.

The man shrugs. 'It's the booby prize. He never liked it here; he spent very little time on this island, though he didn't want his sister Valerie to have it either.'

'Still,' says Sandra, 'it *is* an island, a private island.'

'The others got properties in London and New York and Paris,' says the man. 'I was never his favourite.'

'Why?'

'He wouldn't approve of *this* for example, of me letting

145

half a dozen amateurs come here to fanny about with their second-rate pictures and poems.'

Sandra feels as if she ought to object, but she's not sure on what grounds.

'I'm fully booked through to next summer though,' says the man. 'You're only my first lot.'

'Your guinea pigs,' says Sandra.

'My canaries in a coal mine,' says the man.

'If you own the place, why don't you stay here yourself?' asks Sandra.

'I wouldn't want to live here,' says the man.

'It would be better,' says Sandra, 'with a washer dryer.'

'It's supposed to be basic,' says the man.

'It could at least do with a bigger hot water tank,' says Sandra.

'You're supposed to make sacrifices,' says the man. 'Sacrifice yourself for your art. Comfort is the enemy of progress and all that.'

'I'd be happier if I had a room of my own,' says Sandra. Seeing the look on the man's face, she adds, 'Belle wants a hot tub!' so that he will know her own desires are modest. She thinks of Millet, living in a hut at the edge of a forest in France, barely scraping a living, dedicated to making paintings that were greeted with derision and scorn. Personally, she wants a *certain* amount of comfort. She does not even want to *imagine* a winter without heating – there are limits.

'Anything else?' asks the man, who is leaving now, who is in the doorway.

'I want croissants,' says Sandra, 'and custard tarts.'

The man nods and says he will bring them on Wednesday.

Conscious that time is ticking away, Sandra decides to skip her shower. She goes to get dressed, and discovers the painting clothes she hung over the banisters festering beneath Angie's wet towel. Well, sod it, she thinks, she will go as she is; what does it matter? She just wants to get going.

Outside, a fog is descending, and when she has gone some way it occurs to her that she could do with a torch. There is one in the kitchen. She realises, too, that she has left Colin's containers, his dead creatures, out of the freezer. They will need to be dealt with before they start to smell. She will not go back now.

She presses on. When she reaches the end of the dirt track, she has to go looking for the steps in the cliff, which are not where she remembers. She begins her climb down to the deserted beach, and thinks about the puffins she expected to see; she wonders if they're here after all.

She looks out towards Little Lieloh, which is hard to see through the fog, but which is there nonetheless, and so close.

She walks, with the shingle shifting beneath her feet, to where the rowing boat waits. The knot that ties it to the tree is stubborn and she feels as if she's wearing her fingertips away picking and picking at it. When she finally gets the boat free, moving it takes some effort – it is heavier than she expected – but she manages to get it down the beach and into the water. Trusting it will get her there, she climbs in. She has a feeling of unpreparedness, as she does when she is going away for a while and is trying to think what she might have left undone or unpacked or unlocked; but she is only going this half a mile, no further.

With the oars, she eases herself away from the beach and then out, away from Lieloh.

Even though the conditions seem to be in her favour, getting across is exhausting. On boating lakes, she has covered similar distances quite easily, but the rowing boat feels quite ridiculous at sea, like a bicycle on a motorway. She is determined though, despite the waves that push her off course, that break against the boat and come inside.

By the time she makes it over there, she is aching, and miserably wet. She ties the boat to the jetty. Well, she thinks, it got her here, but she wonders if she is going to make it back. The palm trees that looked so exotic before just look peculiar in the fog.

She has spent years, she thinks, years and years, travelling towards this place, and now she is here. She walks from the shore up a narrowing path, a trail of decaying leaves, ascending towards the white house.

This island cannot be much more than a couple of hundred yards across. She imagines trying to run: she might not have got into her stride on Lieloh, but she wouldn't stand a chance here. She would be forever turning back on herself, like doing lengths of a pool, and even then the house would be in the way. It would be like some hellish combination of the hundred-yard dashes and obstacle courses she was made to do at school.

She can half imagine that beyond this island she might find another, even smaller island. When she was little, she was given a Russian doll, inside which she found another, smaller doll, inside which she found another, even smaller doll. She went on opening the ever shrinking figures until she came to one she could not open, and asked, 'What's inside this one?' Her father, looking at her as if she were an idiot, said, 'Nothing.'

Between her and the house are privet shrubs, trimmed into imposing abstract shapes, like Barbara Hepworths or Henry Moores. Sandra thinks about Valerie's parties, about which Belle was so derisive. She imagines the jack-o'-lanterns guiding the guests along this path and decorating these windows with their terrible grins, everyone in fancy dress, and a general air of splendour. It must have been quite something.

In this gloom, from this angle, the windows look black. She peers in, and sees her own reflection. She thinks of the mirror maze to which she once took Joe. It was confusing: thinking she was speaking to him, moving towards him, she walked into a mirrored wall. Again and again, when she should have been walking towards him, she was walking in another direction altogether, stumbling into her own reflection. You could not tell which way to turn, and you certainly could not run.

From here, she can see the far side of the island, beyond which she can see nothing but sea and fog. She sits down on a bench in the garden. She was planning on working but she is too wet – even her satchel is wet – and her fingers are cold. Also, now that she is actually on the island, she wonders if trying to paint it might be difficult, like trying to see something when you're too close, when you can't see the wood for the trees. She would like, though, seeing as she's here now, to get into the house.

The front door is locked of course, even though such a precaution seems unnecessary when surely hardly anybody ever comes here. Perhaps there is a back door or a ground-floor window that has been overlooked, or she might have to break one of those old windows, though she knows that at least is overstepping a boundary. Setting off around the perimeter, she puts her cold hands into her pockets and feels the keys. She takes them out: the chapel key and an unlabelled key that most likely opens nothing but some dull outbuilding but she sees no harm in trying it.

She does wonder, as she pokes the long key into the old lock, if she might find somebody living here, which would be rather embarrassing. The key not only fits but, with a bit of pressure, turns. It is disconcerting simply to open the door and step into the hallway. 'Hello?' she calls. She looks around, wide-eyed. 'So *this* is Valerie Swanson's house,' she says. It's like being at Graceland, but alone and in the middle of nowhere. There are doors on either side. Behind the first door, she finds a reception room that looks unlived in. Crossing the threshold feels like going behind the rope in a stately home, being where one is not meant to be, touching what is not meant to be touched. The electric lights don't work; she supposes the whole house has been disconnected.

Behind the second door, she finds another reception room, and then a third. The reception rooms are rather soulless. If this were her home, she would want to make some changes. She would want to bring these armchairs closer to the fireplace, although she supposes old chimneys are often blocked up; and she would want to put some pictures on that bare wall, perhaps some local landscapes.

She is horribly uncomfortable in her wet things. Her coat feels cold and heavy. She takes it off and looks for somewhere to hang it, making do with the newel post. She sits down on the stairs to take off her boots. Beneath her damp socks, her feet are wrinkled like an old lady's. She wishes she had brought spare socks, and she could do with that torch; she could do with a little survival kit. She inspects the contents of her wet satchel, the pages of her watercolour pad, the soggy edges of her paintings, which might need cropping.

Barefoot now, soundless on the thick carpet, she ascends the grand staircase. She feels like the lady of the house retiring to her bed.

There is a window on the landing that looks towards Lieloh, towards the shore on which she was so recently standing, beyond the veil of fog, looking this way.

There are more doors here: a whole corridor of bedrooms and bathrooms for a woman who lived here alone. The colour scheme is horrific: one room is red and green, another is purple and yellow. She accepts that the rooms are striking but she could never sleep in a room like that. But if she *had* to, she would choose this one: a room whose bed is right beneath a picture window that looks towards the mainland, not that she could ever see it from here.

And *this*, thinks Sandra, opening the final door at the far end of the corridor, is surely Valerie Swanson's room. The walls are hung with framed posters of silent films in which Valerie Swanson featured. It is like a little museum dedicated to her life. Valerie Swanson was never the star though, and some don't even mention her name. There is a four-poster bed with gold drapes, a gold quilt, gold pillowcases. Sandra can picture Valerie lying there, though she cannot imagine her old: she is frozen in time, shrinking from the horror. Or she can see her reclining on the chaise longue, or sitting at the vanity table, gazing into the mirror – a starlet's bulb-rimmed mirror, the bulbs lit up – picking up the silver-backed hairbrush or opening the silver cigarette case or the silver pill box. There is a chandelier, which is surely too big for a room of this size.

The room smells bad. She has left one foul house behind and arrived in another. It smells like garlic. She goes to the window, pushes it up, and sticks her head out into the fresh air, the sea air, filling her lungs. She finds herself looking for the wild garlic that Belle mentioned, to explain that overwhelming smell, but it's the wrong season for it.

She pulls her head back into the room and turns away to take a look through Valerie's drawers, and as she does so the window slams down behind her, and she thinks *That was close*.

When she has had her fill of the room, she takes one final

look because she won't, she assumes, be here again. She wants to remember it, how beautiful it is. Even the carpet is a dark gold; it is the colour Sandra would want for bracken.

She returns to the ground floor. At the back of the house is a cold kitchen with a big, bare table, and a dresser displaying an empty crackle glaze vase. There is a generous sink, but no running water, and above the sink a window framing the sea. *Water, water everywhere, and not a drop to drink.* A person could not survive here for long.

Just outside is a blackberry bush, and she considers seeing if there are any blackberries left to pick. It's the end of the season but she might find a few if the birds haven't got them. Tomorrow, she could make a crumble to go with the vanilla ice cream, which would surely be appreciated. Beyond the blackberry bush, the garden has largely gone to seed. The vegetable patch is a bright orange eyesore, full of unharvested pumpkins.

She turns away from the window, and sees her shadow, cast against the far wall by the afternoon sun. The pattern on the wallpaper, she notices, is the same as the pattern on her dress, like camouflage, like a landscape in which she could just disappear.

There is a fridge, but it's dead – there's no light, no buzz. She looks in what turns out to be a pantry and finds old food still on the shelves, so many uneaten pumpkin pies left to rot. She thinks, suddenly, about the sandwich that she started on the ferry from Liel and never finished, and which must still be in her rucksack under her bed. There will be mould on it by now; there will be new life growing there.

Also in the pantry are a number of crates of wine. If she were to return to the house with a few bottles of fine wine, vintage wine, the others would no doubt be grateful. She takes hold of a bottle and looks at the label, a handwritten label that says 'elderberry'. She puts the bottle back and closes the pantry door.

Soon, already, the light will start to go. The days are getting shorter and the nights are getting longer and winter will be here before she knows it. She must get going. She must make her way to the jetty and row back, though her arms feel like lead. And will the tide, she wonders, be against her now? It is her turn to wash up, and if she's not there the others will bitch about her. 'All right, I'm leaving now,' she says, as if they can hear her. Anyway, she has seen enough of Valerie Swanson's house, which has its beauty but which is also eerie and rather bleak.

There is one last door that she has not been through, but it is only, she discovers, the door to the cellar, a flight of stairs dropping into darkness. She hesitates on the top step. There is probably not much down there anyway, perhaps more of that mediocre wine.

Thinking she hears something, not in the cellar but behind her, deep in the house, she turns around. 'Hello?' she calls, and waits expectantly.

29

IT IS ALMOST winter and there is frost on the ground. A grand flock of birds flies over and Carol watches them, wondering if they are off somewhere warm, thinking that if they're migrating, they're leaving it late.

One morning, Roman phones to say that he has found a buyer. Carol can stay until the end of the month, maybe longer. 'Unless,' he adds, 'you're ready to leave now?'

'Not quite yet,' says Carol.

'You've not had any more . . . goings-on?' he asks.

'Goings-on?' queries Carol.

'Are they behaving themselves?' asks Roman.

'Who?' asks Carol.

Roman hesitates, and then says, 'Those ghosts of yours,' as if the house were full of them. Carol has taken to calling the ghost 'Miss Swanson', at pains to be polite.

'All quiet on that front,' says Carol.

'All right then,' says Roman. 'I'll leave you to it.'

Carol makes the most of the time she has left. 'I'm working like a madwoman now,' she tells Jayne. Sometimes, she writes through the night. The ending is almost in sight and she is hurtling towards it. It is exhilarating, like driving too fast in the dark.

Finally, one afternoon, she finds she is typing 'THE END'. 'Just like they do in films,' she tells Jayne.

'That must feel good,' says Jayne.

Carol says it does, although in truth she feels a bit like a cartoon character that has run off a cliff, run out of road, and has only just looked down.

'By the way,' says Jayne, 'you know what I said about Lieloh, about an artists' retreat?'

'Yes,' says Carol, who has been rather haunted by that indeterminate accident.

'Well, it turns out that the cellar in which someone died was on *Little* Lieloh, in Valerie Swanson's house.'

'You mean *my* cellar?' says Carol. Still holding the phone to her ear, she moves so that she can see the cellar door, as if she must now keep an eye on it. 'I know it wasn't Valerie, because Valerie died in her bed.' This rather disturbing mystery makes her glad, in the end, that she is leaving.

'I haven't been able to find a name,' says Jayne, but they agree that's neither here nor there.

They make plans to meet up for lunch, somewhere new, and Carol tells Jayne she can't wait. After hanging up, she pours herself a whisky, hoping it will hit the spot. She would have liked to sit and listen to her jazz CDs, which she found eventually, ruined, at the bottom of a bin. After sipping her whisky in silence, and after hitting the last of the golf balls into the sea, she spends the final hour of daylight tackling all sorts of things she has been putting off. She cuts back the privet shrubs lining the path, and the brambles, whose thorns draw blood. In the hallway cupboard, she finds a first aid kit, and a plaster to cover the wound on the pad of her finger, and thinks herself lucky that she has not got to type with it anytime soon.

She makes one last circuit of the house. The shrubs and the brambles will grow again of course, but that will not be her problem.

She is looking forward to an early night. Perhaps in the morning she will wake up with that sense of completion, that sense of satisfaction, that she was expecting to feel. She's already in her nightie; she has not changed out of it for days. Her hair is greasy.

First, she gets in touch with Roman. There is interference on the line but they can just about hear one another. She tells him she has finished her novel.

'You got there in the end,' he says.

'Or at least I've finished the first draft,' she says. She tells him she is ready, now, to leave the house, to go home.

She wonders if she will miss this place, which is, she will admit now – hearing a creak on the stairs, and the slamming of an upstairs door – pretty creepy.

Roman says he can come and fetch her in the morning. 'First thing,' he adds. 'I'll bring breakfast.'

'I'll be ready,' says Carol.

She puts down the phone. She needs to pack, and to make time for at least a quick bath. She must do a spring-clean; the place is a mess and she would not want to leave it that way. And she wants her earlyish night, to be ready to go when Roman arrives in the morning.

And of course, she thinks, as she climbs the stairs, she must tell Miss Swanson that she is leaving. Bracing herself for the garlicky stench, she will knock on the door of that opulent room, and say her goodbyes.

ACKNOWLEDGEMENTS

THANKS TO NICHOLAS Royle, who has now been my agent and editor for more than ten years and who continues to guide, support and encourage my writing. I'm grateful to Jen and Chris Hamilton-Emery at Salt Publishing for their consistent openness to and enthusiasm for my work, and to my ace publicist, Helen Richardson. Thanks to John Oakey, who designs such gorgeous covers for my books and whose positive response to this novel I greatly appreciated. Thanks to my friend Penny Hodson for close reading and generous technical advice, including getting her paints out to check the likelihood of Sandra accidentally getting streaks of white watercolour in her hair. Penny's fine artwork (www. pennyhodson.co.uk) would make Sandra sick with envy. I'm also grateful to my friend Sarah Worrall, who was equally generous with her time and whose feedback was hugely helpful and reassuring. Thanks to Emma King and Dave Norcott who gifted me a subscription to *Oh Comely* magazine, on which I based the arts magazine that Sandra reads. Above all, I'm grateful for the love and support of my husband Dan, whose careful reading of and thoughtful response to my first drafts is always invaluable, and my son Arthur, who is the bee's knees.

I read about 'the island of happiness off the west coast of Ireland' in Robert Macfarlane's *The Old Ways*. The line '*I have had my vision*' is from Virginia Woolf's *To the Lighthouse*. Chapter 9's description of the Lazarus-like red-backed shrike is based on an article by Michael McCarthy in the *Independent*. 'If this isn't nice, I don't know what is' is a Kurt Vonnegut quotation. Sandy's blessing in chapter 22 appears at www. worldprayers.org.

This book has been typeset by
SALT PUBLISHING LIMITED
using Neacademia, a font designed by Sergei Egorov
for the Rosetta Type Foundry in the Czech Republic. It
is manufactured using Holmen Book Cream 70gsm, a
Forest Stewardship Council™ certified paper from the
Hallsta Paper Mill in Sweden. It was printed and bound
by Clays Limited in Bungay, Suffolk, Great Britain.

CROMER
GREAT BRITAIN
MMXXI